T0179782

METAMORPHOSIS

Also by Grist

Afterglow: Climate Fiction for Future Ancestors

METAMORPHOSIS

Climate Fiction for

a Better Future

Introduced by Sheree Renée Thomas

Edited by Grist

MILKWEED EDITIONS

Published 2024 by Milkweed Editions
Printed in Canada
Cover design by Mary Austin Speaker
Cover art by Amelia Bates
24 25 26 27 28   5 4 3 2 1
First Edition

Library of Congress Cataloging-in-Publication Data

Names: Grist, editor.
Title: Metamorphosis : climate fiction for a better future / edited by Grist.
Description: Minneapolis, Minnesota : Milkweed Editions, [2024] | Summary: "A visionary anthology of climate fiction from Grist featuring winning selections from Grist's Imagine 2200 short story contest"-- Provided by publisher.
Identifiers: LCCN 2024006356 (print) | LCCN 2024006357 (ebook) | ISBN 9781571311498 (trade paperback) | ISBN 9781571311542 (ebook)
Subjects: LCSH: Climatic changes--Fiction. | Science fiction, American--21st century. | Short stories, American--21st century. | LCGFT: Climate fiction. | Science fiction. | Short stories.
Classification: LCC PS648.C55 M48 2024 (print) | LCC PS648.C55 (ebook) | DDC 813/.608036--dc23/eng/20240725
LC record available at https://lccn.loc.gov/2024006356
LC ebook record available at https://lccn.loc.gov/2024006357

Milkweed Editions is committed to ecological stewardship. We strive to align our book production practices with this principle, and to reduce the impact of our operations in the environment. We are a member of the Green Press Initiative, a nonprofit coalition of publishers, manufacturers, and authors working to protect the world's endangered forests and conserve natural resources. *Metamorphosis* was printed on acid-free 100% postconsumer-waste paper by Friesens Corporation.

Contents

Editor's Note

In a world filled with deep divisions and terrifying climate disasters, it's easy to lose hope. But what if we could use our imaginations to create a different future? This book you're reading, a collection of stories from Grist's Imagine 2200: Climate Fiction for Future Ancestors project, is a portal, a map, and a springboard for exploring how fiction can help create a better reality. It is also an invitation to join us in collective dreaming about what it means to ensure a better future for all.

Grist is a nonprofit, independent media organization dedicated to telling stories of climate solutions and a just future. We're known for our award-winning reporting that illuminates the inequitable impacts of the climate crisis and the work being done to mitigate its effects. With Imagine 2200, we aim to bring to life those creative climate solutions and community-centered adaptations through fictional works that look beyond the current moment and inspire both readers and writers to imagine a world where climate justice is a reality.

Since 2021, the Imagine 2200 project, through a short story contest, has dared writers across the globe to imagine a world where humanity has healed its relationship with nature and one another, vanquished the climate crisis, and built worlds that have upended the status quo of colonialism, extraction, and oppression. Nearly three thousand people from one hundred countries have submitted stories that elevate diverse voices and bring new perspectives to the increasingly vital genre of climate fiction.

This anthology represents a selection of recent winners and finalists. In it you will find writers of all ages, races, ethnicities, genders, and backgrounds, each offering different visions of what it means to be hopeful and what a better world looks like. Their stories explore a wide range of possibilities, from technological advancements to cultural shifts, all the while unapologetically celebrating the cultures and identities of their characters.

Although these stories are mostly about the future, our hope is that they will influence the present by helping all of us envision the world we want.

TORY STEPHENS
Grist Climate Fiction Creative Manager

Introduction

A Memory of the Future

Otherworldly but remarkably familiar, interdimensional but set right *here*, ancestral but firmly rooted in alternate futures, the stories gathered here encircle us with possibility. Written by writers from around the globe, these original tales power us forward through present challenges to bravely face hard truths and seek other solutions.

What makes these works noteworthy is that, despite their foundation in the genre of the impossible, they do not end with the well-worn and disheartening belief that all roads lead to, and all stories must end in, dystopia. They offer hope and faith in our ability as an imperfect but resilient species to unpack past traumas, discard old beliefs and traditions that no longer serve us, and embrace community wherever we are fortunate enough to find, build, and nurture it.

Though we share space in a time when some of the world's most impactful societies and leaders have made choices that are deeply unsettling, some of those choices made generations ago, these stories remind us that as long as we rise under the light of the distant sun, there is still a chance for us to revisit the wisdom of the elders. There is still a chance to compare notes and study the successes of those who have chosen other intentional paths, so that we may become better stewards of the world we cherish— and one another.

These works not only offer alternate ways of seeing but also are rooted in time-honored storytelling techniques that engage us through deep characterization, vivid world-building, image-laden prose, and story arcs that empower even as they take us to the brink—and then carry us on past self-doubt, despair, apathy, and resignation to the realms of positive imagination.

There are no easy answers here, only intersections of ideas and other choices that can, have been, and could be made. For it is the call for a deeper, more humane, and radical imagining that is required of us to meet the challenges of the day.

Climate fiction—the genre of stories you're about to read—is vital to the world's work because it offers us opportunities to personally engage and connect to these overwhelming concepts in a safe and limitless space: the imagination. When that imagination is engaged toward positive futures, it gives us power. A positive, radical imagination is the difference between those who still believe and those who stand still and no longer seek solutions or other ways of being because they have already accepted that we have lost—those who believe there is nothing we can do individually and collectively to reverse course and protect ecologies and biospheres, our homes and our communities, from the devastation of climate change.

When we bring to that imagining the wisdom of our elders,

and meet our ancestral intelligence—the first AI—with our collective minds to explore the concerns of the present, as in Afrofuturism, Indigenous futurism, queer futurism, and other liberated futurisms, we can build and heal ourselves. This intentional focus frees us all to create powerful experiential futures that reflect our best selves. And it is our best selves that we want most to survive into the future, our boldest, coldest, wildest, and most expansive, humane, loving dreams.

To live in the futures we dream of requires not just breath, body, and blood, water and sustenance, but unwavering courage to reexamine our worldviews, values, and cultures, the systems we engage with, and our relationship to the land and all that lives on Earth. This work of excavation is necessary to create space for new ideas, new ranges of motion and emotion, and new stories for the real-time cultural and personal change that is needed for us to survive and thrive together beyond this crisis of nature and commerce, of humanity's destructive global economies that have made a nightmare of our relationship to the land and each other.

What these original stories remind us, like young activists such as Vanessa Nakate, Eric Marky, Helena Gualinga, Yurshell Rodriguez, Cécile Ndjebet, Portia Adu-Mensah, Bright Toh, Elizabeth Wathuti, and so many more who are living on the front lines of the climate crisis, is that climate change is not just an abstract existential crisis. It is a present and lived reality with consequences for us all. The future requires an unshakable memory, positive engagement, courage, and a radical imagination. Nothing less will do.

And this is a rare gem of an experience, to immerse oneself in a collection of science fiction, climate fiction tales that reject nihilism and the belief that humanity's demise is inevitable. It is a kind of magic, a strange alchemy for such disparate writers to skillfully create memorable works that occupy distinctive spaces in the science fiction and fantasy genres but are in deep conversation with each other. Entering the world of one tale provides an opportunity for reflection on the layers of another.

These works recognize the cosmic forces in the universe and the memories embedded in the natural world. Designed not just to entertain but also to illuminate and transform, the stories in this collection reenergize. Sometimes, when our minds are enveloped in the fog of pessimism, we become almost spirit, lifted away by fear. It takes energy to push away the weight of indifference, to see past the dire headlines that announce it's too late to make significant change in the climate crisis, which is to say our culture crisis, and to drown out the cynical news stories and sound bites so that we can hear the voices of the earth.

We may have nothing to teach the wind, the waters, and the sky, but they have much to teach us. The writers of *Metamorphosis: Climate Fiction for a Better Future* remind us that we all must listen beyond mortal language, beyond the language of fear, and reach for that elemental brightness, that radical imagining that is a memory of the future. A future that gleams with the most furious love.

SHEREE RENÉE THOMAS

METAMORPHOSIS

The Metamorphosis of Marie Martin

Nadine Tomlinson

When her eyes were at her knees and Mama was teaching her how to swim, she told her that drowning is easy and staying alive is the realest struggle. But she was a *pickney* then, so the words did go through one ear and fly out the other. They fly back in again when she got pregnant at almost fifteen and drop out of high school. Now, they come back, wheeling around in her head like John Crows.

So this is what it feel like fi dead.

She's a rock, sinking. Part of her know she mustn't drop asleep.

—Sleep is the sister of Death, Boysie did say.

Swim back to the shore.

She has to go back home. But her body not cooperating at all. It behaving like a hard ears pickney, just like what Mama used to call her.

Something not right. *How mi feel so light, like mi weigh likkle and nothing?*

Mama used to boast about her: "Yuh see my Bubbles? Don't watch her size. She can do anything—climb coconut tree, *kin pupalick*, do splits—even though she fat. She better than seven sons. Heh! Bet *oonu* never know she was swimming like fish before she could walk."

She can't feel her legs. She looks down.

They're not there. Like the rest of her body.

She drew Precious into her arms, ran her hand over her hair with its neat canerows, straight and smooth, unlike the roads in Ackee Town that full of potholes. Once, a taxi man told her that if your vehicle make mistake and drop into one, you would end up in China.

"Precious, stop cry now. I soon come back." She held her at arm's length, brushed stray tears away.

"Miss Cunningham said eagle fishing—"

"Illegal."

"Illegal fishing is wrong, and overfishering—"

"Overfishing."

"Overfishing is bad 'cause there won't be any fish left." Precious stopped, trying to remember. "And the crawls need the fish to keep them clean and healthy."

"Corals."

"Yes, Mummy. Mummy, you nuh 'fraid fi go prison?"

"Precious, what ah tell yuh 'bout speaking Patwah?"

"But you do it all the time."

This chile. "Yes, but I know when to speak it. Nothing is wrong with Patwah, but I want you to practice speaking Standard

English because"—she glanced at Sweets as she approached and stood at the entrance to the bedroom—"I want a better life for you. This is 2032, but some people will still judge you by how yuh talk. Don't make your mouth hold yuh back in life. And yuh auntie and me not going to prison, so stop worry. We not hurting anybody, baby. We trying to survive. Listen, sometimes you have to do things that people say are wrong for a good cause." She kissed her forehead. "You are my good cause."

"Come, Bubbles." Sweets clicked her tongue, patted her speargun. "We haffi go now." She headed toward the front door.

Precious started bawling again. "Mummy, don't go. *Please.*"

"Marley, stop it! Yuh finish yuh homework?"

Precious's tears slowly dried up like the taps during water lock-offs. Her eyes round like a dinner plate, the way she surprised. "Mummy, you said my name."

Same time, Mama rushed into the room as if she heard bad news. "What happen to har?" She moved closer to Precious and rested the back of her hand against her neck and forehead. "She never use to behave like dis when you go fishing."

She stood up, smoothed away the creases her backside made on the bedspread. "I don't know, Mama, and I haffi leave now."

"Come, *putus.*" Mama gently led Precious out of the room.

In the kitchen, Mama took a jar of nutmegs out of a cupboard and put one in Precious's mouth to soothe her nerves. She screwed up her face but obeyed Mama when she told her not to spit it out and to sit at the dining room table.

Mama handed her a clean sheet of loose paper and her box of crayons. "Draw somet'ing nice fi yuh Mummy."

Precious nodded and set to work. Mama pushed out her lips to indicate that they should go outside.

In the front yard, Sweets was sitting on the concrete staircase beside the house.

"God go wid oonu. Remember de offering fi Boysie."

Sweets shook her head, sighed. "Mama, why yuh must say the same t'ing every time we go fishing? We always do it."

"He was mi only son. I want him to continue rest in peace."

"Mummy, wait." Precious ran toward her, waving the loose sheet of paper like a flag.

"How yuh finish draw so quick? What yuh do wid de nutmeg?" Mama pretended to look stern.

"It on de—" She stopped, remembering. "It's on the table. I'm okay now, Grandma." She turned to her. "This is for you, Mummy."

She took the paper, grinned at the drawing of a silver-and-blue-and-pink fish with her name under it. "Thanks, baby. It's really pretty." She handed it back to her. "Ask Grandma for a magnet, so yuh can put it on de fridge." She squatted to give her a quick hug. "Auntie and me going to bring back nuff parrotfish and snapper, okay?"

"I'm going to stop eating parrotfish."

"Why? It's your favorite."

"Miss Cunningham said not a lot of fish are left."

"Miss Cunningham is a teacher, not a fisherwoman."

"She invited a marie blygist to class last week."

"Marine biologist."

"Yes, Mummy. The lady said parrotfish can save the beaches and crawls—the corals. She said sand comes from parrotfish doo-doo." Her expression changed, as if she had the whole world balancing on her six-year-old shoulders. "Mummy, please don't catch any more parrotfish. You can help them."

"Precious, I . . ." She pinched the bridge of her nose, let her hand fall into her lap. "Behave yuhself and listen to Grandma. We soon come back."

As she shifted to straighten herself, Precious grabbed her arm and pulled her down to her level again. She whispered in her ear, pivoted like a ballet dancer, and sprinted like Usain Bolt inside the house.

"Bubbles! Bubbles!" Mama's voice echoed as if from inside a tunnel. "Sweets, move fast and bring de bottle of white rum mek mi rub some on har face. She look like she gwine collapse!"

⁂

She want to scream, to put down a piece of cow-bawling and roll on the ground, but her new mouth feel like it belong to a stranger. *No, Jah. This can't be real.* In the broken glass bottom of a boat that cotch on a damaged coral reef, her shattered reflection make her feel like she going mad.

Mighty God of Daniel, as Mama would say.

Her silver-and-gray parrotfish reflection stare back at her.

How dis happen to mi? Why it happen to mi? Mi can turn back into miself? How mi going to get back home?

Tears and rage building up inside her like a Category 5 storm, but she have no way to let them out. Every time life kick her down, she kick back as good as she got.

Now, mi can't even give it one good kick, to rahtid.

The words Precious whispered to her fly back in her ear.

No, she can't give up. Her body is different now, but she's still Marie Martin, Melba's daughter, Sweets's sister, and Precious's mother. She's a hustler. A survivor. Tough and stubborn to break like jackass corn. As much as she want to bawl her eyes out, common sense is taking over and telling her she has to survive in this new world. What would Mama say?

"Bubbles, if yuh know what good fi yuh, yuh better think like a fish."

Is nighttime, so moray eels are hunting parrotfish. Instead of being the hunter, she's now the prey. She need to find somewhere to—

What is this now? Trouble always set like rain.

Ten, fifteen, likkle more than twenty parrotfish coming toward her. Right off the bat, she know which one is the don. Living in Ackee Town teach you these things. He's full bodied and look *boasy* in pink and electric blue. Something jump inside her like it frighten. Guilt seize her. She wish she could tell him sorry. His eyes walk all over her while the others circle her like they investigating a crime scene. Next thing she know, they nudging her. She gear up herself to fight, bite, until she sense they want her to follow them.

Jah, where them taking mi?

All of them moving like one body. She in the middle, somehow managing to keep up. Even though she shooting through the water faster than Alia Atkinson, and feel water leaving her gills to merge with the sea, she not thirsty. The seawater feel smooth like cocoa butter as it slide over her gills. The liquid air in this blue-green world is sweet like ripe Julie mangoes bursting in her mouth, the golden juice running down to her elbow, now a memory.

Her new eyes allow her to see all around her at the same time. They not burning or watering, no matter how long she stare, because she don't need to blink. The seawater is as invisible to her as the air when she walked on land. She and the other parrotfish moving like colorful light over a field of waving seagrass. Around a bend, she almost collide with a bleached coral reef squatting like a tenement yard. The corals stare back at her like the discolored faces of misguided young men and women in her community, who believe that lightening their dark complexion is a ladder out of the pit of poverty.

Two-twos, they reach a healthy reef. She and Sweets never dive in this section. It's like a brand-new world, full of color and life. A clownfish hide among some staghorn corals when it spot her. *Wait! Is a sea turtle dat? Can't tell when last mi see one.* The baby fish peep at her from the reef's crevices. Some more parrotfish, along with a handful of snappers, watching her.

Dem know mi different? Why dem help mi?

She's an outsider. Before her change, she was their enemy. A predator.

Something happening to her again.

Is what dis slimy substance on mi body? Yuck!

It's on the other parrotfish too. They settling down for the night in the nooks and crannies of the reef.

Ohhh! The slime hide us from predators.

She find a crevice, slip into it, and watch them. Sleep biting her, but she fighting it. She look to her right. The leader's eye and her own make two.

Is like him read mi mind and know mi don't plan to stay here.

Quick-quick, she form like she sleeping.

Maybe mi will turn back into miself once mi reach de shore.

First chance she get, she out of here.

�֍

The sea, so quiet, unlike inside her. Precious's words tumbling over and over in her head like when she kin pupalick. The sky was a black sheet that the moon hiding behind. Sweets's mouth moving as she poured libations into the seawater. When she finished her ritual, she lit a spliff and blew perfect *O*'s toward the black sheet above, just like Boysie's habit before he began fishing for the day or night. He used to say that was how him feel the power of their ancestors guiding him. She always wondered if he smoked that day when he died.

Sweets nudged her foot with hers. "Your time."

She leaned over the side of the *Empress of the Sea* and placed a calabash containing trimmings from their hair and nails, along with another calabash filled with white rice and curry goat, on the back of the seawater. Ripple by ripple, the water carried them away.

"Mikayla, promise me somet'ing."

"Whatever it is, it must be serious. Can't tell when last mi hear yuh call me by mi government name."

"Promise me you'll look after Precious if anyt'ing happen to me."

"Stop chat faat. Me an' Mama not doing dat a'ready?"

"I mean . . . be her mother. *You*."

"What happen to yuh tonight? How yuh sound like yuh spooked?"

"Just promise me an' done, nuh?" She kissed her teeth.

"All right, all right. Nuh bodda get ignorant pon me. Of course. Yuh never haffi ask." She outed the spliff between her thumb and forefinger and sucked them. "Yuh ready?" She put on her mask and fins and took up her speargun.

"Right behind you." She attached a dive flashlight to the lanyard around her wrist and turned it on. "Ten minutes?"

"Nine." Sweets slipped beneath the skin of the seawater like a whisper.

She ignored the needle prick in her conscience when they reached a no-take zone.

Suppose de wardens catch you and Sweets?

What yuh expect we fi do? Look how much wages we lose sake o' de sanctuary's restrictions. How mi must help put food on de table, plus pay Precious's school fees an' buy her holo-textbooks if mi nuh do dis?

So what you going to do when no more fish are left?

Sweets's hand signal distracted her just in time. She squashed the whispers in her head. Then almost forgot to keep holding her breath. A flash of the brightest blue she ever saw. The water can play tricks on your mind when your body doing its best to conserve oxygen. But she wasn't seeing things. A pretty electric-blue–and–neon-pink parrotfish side-eyeing them like him want to know what their business is around these parts. The speargun suddenly felt heavy in her hand. Her fingers curled around it tighter than usual. She needed the money bad-bad. Sweets gave her the thumbs-up sign. She aimed at the pretty parrotfish. Before she could shoot, it darted away.

Too late, she understood why.

A giant moray eel.

Before she or Sweets could react, it latched onto Sweets's leg. She started doing the one thing she shouldn't do.

—Panic kill first before de drowning, Boysie did say when he was teaching them to free dive.

Alarm bells like police sirens in her head. She turned her head just in time to see a goliath grouper charging toward her.

—Sometimes dem work together, Boysie did say. De enemy of mi enemy is mi friend.

Sweets taking in more water.

Nine minutes.

Boysie used to hold out until eleven minutes. But she and Sweets not that good.

She aimed at the grouper.

What she did expect? Going back didn't change a thing. She's still a parrotfish. The taste of disappointment is bitter in her mouth as if she swallowed cerasee tea.

By now, her family must think she dead. She can't imagine what they going through, especially Mama. She and Precious took it extremely hard when Boysie died last year. Now, they going to have to deal with the pain of losing her.

Something inside her like a long piece of rope is pulling her toward the reef with the fish. The other end is hauling her heart toward Ackee Town and her family. After dillydallying in her mind, she make a U-turn with a heavy feeling inside. Might as well go back. It not safe to be out here alone.

The bleached coral reef still look an old tenement yard. The last time she saw a forest of beautiful, healthy reefs was when she was eight years old. Precious isn't that fortunate. She has to depend on her science holo-textbook and visor to see moving 4D images of coral reefs when they were in their glory.

But stop! Why she so focused on the past? She was always a person to look forward, to plan for whatever was waiting around the corner. Just because she's a fish now don't mean that part of her change. She was just sleeping in a healthy reef, which means that there's hope for this one and others like it. She could help the other parrotfish to restore the reefs and beaches. Precious and the children in Ackee Town could get to see a thriving reef for real and play on a beach one day. She couldn't change back and return to her family, but she could do something for them and the land she left behind that would benefit them now and throughout the coming years.

You have to say goodbye to your old life and accept your new one. You can do that?

I can do anything fi mi family. Mi want good fi dem, so mi nose haffi run.

Your new family waiting for you. Hurry up.

She sense it even before she reach. Not one of them is sleeping. They move as one toward her and form a circle around her. Sound waves sliding off their bodies. She understand them. They wondering where she did go. If she could bawl, she would. She only experienced that kind of care and concern from Mama, Boysie, Sweets, and Precious.

Inside her feel like knots unraveling. Instinct take over and she start to vibrate just like them. She going to tell them everything.

She can almost hear Mama's cheerful, hoarse laugh.

"Come, mi dear. Mek we lap frock tail. Mi have one story fi gi' yuh!"

The air never tasted so sweet before. She gulped it, choked, gulped some more. Her eyes burned like when you make mistake and take your hand that have Scotch bonnet pepper juice on it and rub your eye.

She could barely feel her arms as she hauled Sweets toward the *Empress of the Sea.*

"Sweets. Sweets! Yuh hear mi?"

She coughed. Nodded. Cried out when she tried to climb into the boat.

"After three. One, two, three." She strained to push Sweets up and over into the boat.

Sweets coughed again, sat up. Pain all over her face as she looked at the wound on her leg.

"Yuh going need stitches. No clinic is open at this time o' night."

Sweets rummaged through the first aid kit. "Mi will ask Mama to sew it up when we reach back." Her hands trembled as she cleaned the cut.

"De timing bad, but mi soon come back."

Sweets's head snapped up. "Where yuh going?"

"To get de spearguns."

"Leff dem. It nuh worth it."

"How we going manage without them?"

"Mi a beg yuh. Nuh go back down there. Mek we go home."

"Yuh know how much money fi one speargun, not to mention two?"

Sweets coughed, spat.

"Mi nah tek long. Three minutes max."

She slipped beneath the rippling seawater before Sweets could form another word.

Two minutes.

The spearguns were right where she and Sweets dropped them. Her flashlight flickered.

No no no!

She knocked it two times. The light jerked on, off, on . . .

She dived quick-quick, grabbed the spearguns.

. . . off.

A cramp shoot up her right leg like a lightning bolt.

She forgot to breathe, dropped the flashlight and the spearguns. Pain forced her mouth open.

Four minutes.

She should've listened to Sweets. Her tired muscles felt like a rubber band that stretch out till it slack. She fighting the water and reaching nowhere fast. Only losing air like a tire with a leak.

In her ears, her heart was a slow drumbeat from far away.

She was a rock, sinking.

Her body jerked once, twice.

She landed on something rough. Dimly, she realized it was a dying coral reef.

So this is what it feel like fi dead.

Her body sank into the bed of corals.

Before everything went black, her last memory was of Precious grabbing her arm and whispering in her ear, "You're not coming back, Mummy, but you're not going to die."

What is time now? It fly like a hummingbird. She learn to mark it by the shape of the moon. Thirteen moons show their round faces since the last night she walked on two legs. The feeling of missing her human body is a memory. Everything from that time is a dream now.

The little girl in a blue dress with pink flowers is running barefoot to the beach's hairline. What she name again? Precious. She used to miss her. That ache is lost in a distant memory. She get taller, but she still skinny like bamboo. Well, that not changing. She get her size from her father. She holding a sheet of paper close to her chest. Her eyes searching the water. Six moons she been doing the same thing.

A fat woman with hair like thin ropes the color of the rainbow is heading toward the little gi—Precious. *Try remember her name. It won't be long before she's just another little girl on a beach.* The woman . . . she name . . . Sweets. She say something to Precious that make her face light up a bit, like when a cloud can't hide the sun's smile.

Some people are arriving in twos, threes, fours. Not the ones she have to be careful of. The ones who try to catch her and her family. No, these people, some with dark faces, others paler, come to swim or eat or lie down on the beach, now that there are beaches on the island again and seafood restaurants are back in business. She don't spot the ones who came a whole heap of times to examine and test the sand on this beach. They were excited can't done, as if it was the first time they were seeing sand. Sand that came from her and her family. Special sand that she helped to create.

An older woman is coming toward Precious and Sweets. Mama. Her hair is more salt than pepper. Her body look like it's holding up her dress. That face used to know belly laughing and smiles. It's strange to see her here today. The last time she step foot here was when the sand returned, six moons ago.

Movement beside her. She never have to look to see that it's the electric-blue–and–neon-pink parrotfish. He started joining her whenever she came to check if Precious, Sweets, and Mama on the beach. She wonder if he remember them. She wonder how long it took him to forget that he was Boysie.

Is the sand did make her realize he was her brother. The same sand on the beach that caused those strangers to get excited. Her and Boysie's doo-doo is different. Boysie smart, so she feel he figured it out too.

Precious step into the seawater with purpose, her eyes seeking something. Finally, she bend down and let a gentle wave carry the paper away. Six moons she been doing the same thing. Each time, her face would screw up and water would spill from her eyes like rain. Same thing happen again. She turn and run to Sweets, who kneel down on the sand and hug her. Mama trying to stand up strong, but she look like she going to keel over any minute.

She wish she could tell them that the sea gives more than she takes. That what was lost is found. That in her previous life, she took more than she gave, but everything is balanced now because she gave the biggest gift of her entire existence, past and present. She, Boysie, and their offspring helped to restore this beach, and others on the island, better than they were before. She wish she could tell them that what was given up as dead is reborn. She wish she could show them the coral reefs, stronger than before, like underwater rainforests filled with countless fish and other sea creatures. She wish she could say, "All is not lost. Dat sand oonu standing on is hope. It will bear oonu up today, tomorrow, and for the rest of oonu lives."

The special sand is the greatest gift she, Boysie, and their offspring can offer them from their bodies. When her and his time come, they will leave behind a strong and lasting legacy. This island and others in the Caribbean can finally exhale in relief.

More people show up, spreading over the beach like ants. She can't see Precious, Sweets, and Mama anymore. By the next ripe moon, she might forget the blood tie she once shared with them, and think of them as strangers she recognized. Even Boysie will become just a pretty parrotfish to her one day.

As if he read her mind, he nudge her to make her know is time to leave. For a moment, as she look at him, Boysie's shoulder-length dreadlocks and a smile like pearls in his long, dark face flash behind her eyes. Somehow, she know she would never see it again after today. But it's okay. They're together again, even when they won't remember who they were to each other in a yesterday life.

The flash behind her eyes fading like when the evening sun slowly dipping into the sea. But not before Boysie grin and say in his husky voice, "Come, Bubbles. Mek we go home now."

To Labor for the Hive

Jamie Liu

Huaxin always took pride in telling people she met her partner while doing tai chi in the park. Every other young person nowadays found their relationships through AI matchmaking services or VR mixers. But Huaxin was old-fashioned.

She'd joined the crew of elders practicing, their moves fluid as the stream that ran by the village. She'd spotted him then, the only other face as young as hers: a thin man with glasses, thick curls of hair, and a gentle smile. Naturally, they'd felt drawn to each other, and Huaxin struck up a conversation.

After that, they met up for tea following each tai chi session. He was a lot like Huaxin: opinionated, particular, averse to vulnerability. He was also impulsive. He picked up new topics easily, researched them with relish, and constantly talked to her about how the world was changing.

One day he led her back to the park and removed a ring from his pocket. It was no diamond, but Huaxin still gasped when she saw it: a smooth stone, well-worn like a comforting friend. "The world may be changing," he said with a cheeky grin, "but I want you to be my constant."

He moved in with her, and she introduced him to her livelihood: beehousing. They shared bowls of noodles, talked about having children, and continued to practice tai chi, nurturing their slowly aging bodies.

And then, nine years later, he left her.

"And why do you need this information again?" Huaxin snapped into the phone.

"Science," the person on the other end said. This was the third time Huaxin had asked, and now it seemed like the man was going for the simplest explanation possible. "It'll provide useful data to prevent natural disasters. We know your region is highly flood prone. This will help you prepare for that."

Huaxin chewed her lip. Did they know how her parents had died? If so, of course they'd come running to her. "And you're saying the bees will provide this data?"

"Yes. Just click on the link I sent you. Again, I'd like to offer our services to install digital monitoring systems in the hives. It'll be completely free and will make it easier—"

"No thanks," Huaxin said, hanging up. On her computer, she clicked on the unread message.

They wanted her to download an app. Didn't she have enough shit clogging up her phone? Wasn't there an option to just send an email with whatever observations they wanted her to make? She clicked the Support button and typed: *i don't want your fucking app*

Huaxin's phone buzzed. She'd received a text.

SUPPORT: *Hey there, can you explain your dilemma to me?*

Huaxin eyed the screen in suspicion. Was this an automated response? Or worse, AI? She didn't want to talk to a robot.

HUAXIN: *are you a human?*

SUPPORT: *Yes, I am.*

HUAXIN: *who are you?*

SUPPORT: *I'm a scientist with Sichuan Resilient. I help implement the nature-based early warning system we've partnered with the Beijing Office of Meteorology on. Is that what you're asking about today?*

HUAXIN: *i guess*

SUPPORT: *May I ask why you don't want to download our app?*

HUAXIN: *too many apps on my phone*

SUPPORT: *I understand. Do you prefer another method of reporting data?*

HUAXIN: *can i just email it to someone*

SUPPORT: *You can email it to me.*

The scientist sent Huaxin an email address, and Huaxin breathed a sigh of relief.

HUAXIN: *thanks*

HUAXIN: *what's your name*

SUPPORT: *My name is Anshui. You are Huaxin Lin, correct?*

HUAXIN: *mhm*

HUAXIN: *so the guy on the phone said i'll get paid for this?*

SUPPORT: *Yes. Think of it like a part-time job. We know it takes time out of your day to record these observations and send them to us, so we want to make sure you're compensated.*

HUAXIN: *i still don't know how bees will help prevent flooding*

SUPPORT: *Several studies show that some species of animals, including bees, exhibit specific behaviors prior to an extreme weather event. This program is two-fold: by telling us how the bees are behaving, we can predict if something like a flood is going to happen, and we can distribute emergency messaging to your region. On the research side, if we collect enough data that connects certain bee behavior to weather events, we'll have more ways of predicting disasters in the future.*

HUAXIN: *you're telling me you can't predict floods already with your fancy science tools?*

SUPPORT: *With the unpredictable ways climate events are unfolding, meteorological stations can do only so much. We're testing supplemental methods by using nature–based solutions. Nature is very wise; we just have to listen.*

HUAXIN: *sounds like some hippie bullshit to me*

SUPPORT: *We're included in that nature. Doesn't your body sometimes tell you when it's going to rain?*

That was true. If Huaxin didn't smell it in the air, she literally felt it in her bones. She'd brought it up to a doctor once, who told her that sometimes people with joint issues could feel pressure changes in their knees. She didn't like the idea of having weak joints. She was thirty-seven, hardly ancient.

HUAXIN: *i guess*

SUPPORT: *If you have any other questions, please let me know.*

SUPPORT: *Have a nice day :)*

This person seemed like they had the role of a customer service representative plus IT person. Basically, the worst job ever. She put her phone away and went outside.

It was spring. From her home in the hills, Huaxin could see cracks of color speckling into view as new buds bloomed across the valley. The bees stirred from their slumber, buzzing more than they had in the previous months.

Over the years, Huaxin had departed from her family's traditional beekeeping and veered into beehousing, an emerging practice that was more about providing for bees' needs than managing bees. She still had one Chinese honeybee hive, but she'd also dotted her garden with bee motels, plant matter, and soil mounds to serve as wild bee habitats. Similarly, she'd filled her garden with a diverse mix of native plants: sweetly fragrant lychee and peach trees, traditional Chinese medicine staples like black cardamom and butterfly bush, native pea shrub and milk vetch, and vegetables like sponge gourd and radish.

Other than harvesting honey, Huaxin didn't "keep" any of the bees. Certainly not the wild ones. She provided them shelter and food, and they pollinated her plants. The bees were gentle with her. She liked this relationship; it was easy to understand. Give respect and receive respect in return. It wasn't the same with humans.

After collecting data, she sipped homemade jasmine tea with a dollop of honey and took out her phone.

HUAXIN: *6am, roughly 50 bees per hive en route to flowers, determined dance, will report on return times in afternoon*

SUPPORT: *Thank you.*

SUPPORT: *You can send me one report at the end of the day if you prefer, rather than multiple throughout.*

HUAXIN: *i won't remember all the details if i do that*

HUAXIN: *would you rather me not text you every hour*

SUPPORT: *No, this is fine.*

SUPPORT: *Determined dance, I like that.*

HUAXIN: *thinking of their routes as dances helps me characterize them*

HUAXIN: *sometimes it's a lion dance, sometimes it's tai chi*

HUAXIN: *anyway you're right, i don't want to bother you with notifications*

SUPPORT: *I don't mind. I like the frequent texts. I don't get a lot of messages.*

That was . . . sad. Or maybe not? Maybe it meant Anshui had a rich social life completely offline. That sounded amazing.

HUAXIN: *aren't you texting other bee people*

SUPPORT: *They're not all beekeepers. And most of them use the app, which automates the data delivery.*

HUAXIN: *ah so i'm just a high-maintenance bitch*

SUPPORT: *You like doing things your way, which I admire.*

Something tingled in Huaxin's stomach. She bit her lip.

HUAXIN: *are you flirting with me*

SUPPORT: *. . . No. Apologies if it came across that way.*

SUPPORT: *I can stop if you want.*

SUPPORT: *Texting you things unrelated to the data monitoring, I mean.*

Huaxin didn't know what to say, so she stashed her phone.

The rest of the day was like any other, with the addition of her data duties. She tended to her garden. She visited the porch when people rang to buy her products. She made lunch: yellow squash from her garden, stir-fried with fermented black beans and tofu from the weekly market. She texted updates to Anshui, who didn't respond until the end of the day with a "thank you."

Someone knocked on the door. The sun had set by now, so Huaxin already knew who it was. "Hi, Ms. Chen. The usual?"

Ms. Chen gave a curt nod. "And two lychee honey sticks, please. Need something to drown out the medicine tonight."

Huaxin nodded, fetching the jars and sticks. Ms. Chen was her older neighbor—well, if one counted a neighbor as someone who lived two hills away. She'd lived a nocturnal life ever since she lost her job decades ago when countrywide protests caused the country to shut down its last coal mines. Their little town had celebrated. Ms. Chen had not. With no family, she'd taken pride in her work and found her purpose lost after that work disappeared. She'd lived in isolation ever since, except to visit town every once in a while to grab groceries or buy honey from Huaxin.

Huaxin felt a kinship with her.

"Hot today," Ms. Chen said as she took the honey. Their few exchanges of conversation had to do with the weather. As it was with people who never talked to others.

"Yeah."

"I hope it was worth it."

"Sorry?"

Ms. Chen gazed into the distance. "Shutting down the mines. I hope it helped. The heat would be worse, right?"

Oh. She was talking about climate change. Huaxin always avoided the topic with Ms. Chen. It was the global effort to decarbonize that had lost her her job, after all. And yes, shutting down the coal mines was a good thing. But the government had not made sure she'd had another livelihood to jump to after the transition.

Still, it wasn't bitterness in Ms. Chen's voice. Instead there was . . . guilt? Regret?

No. Ms. Chen's eyes were watery. She'd been forgotten. Abandoned. She wanted to know her abandonment was worth it. It wasn't the income she would have missed the most; the country's social programs meant no one needed to work to survive. But Huaxin knew that for Ms. Chen, her job had also provided her a sense of routine, of camaraderie. Ms. Chen mourned the loss of that.

"Yes," Huaxin said. "It would be worse."

⁑

The next morning, Huaxin woke up feeling empty. She texted Anshui.

HUAXIN: *hi*

HUAXIN: *you can talk to me*

HUAXIN: *i don't want this to be weird*

SUPPORT: *Okay, thank you.*

SUPPORT: *Sorry again.*

HUAXIN: *don't apologize*

HUAXIN: *how did you sleep*

SUPPORT: *Not bad. It was warm but I have good AC. You?*

HUAXIN: *no good AC but i'm used to the heat*

HUAXIN: *gonna get started on the bees now, will report in a bit*

She went through the motions faster today and poured herself another cup of tea before going back to her phone.

HUAXIN: *6:15am bee workday start. lazy bastards. 40 bees per hive, more like tai chi*

SUPPORT: *The bees deserve to rest too.*

HUAXIN: *i'm joking. i like bees more than humans*

SUPPORT: *What's wrong with humans?*

HUAXIN: *we made the mess that's making you have to do this whole early warning thing, right?*

HUAXIN: *selfishly polluting and not caring about nature*

SUPPORT: *We also realized our mistakes and put ourselves on the path to healing the planet. Isn't that a good redemption arc?*

Huaxin recoiled. Some people didn't deserve a redemption arc. But she couldn't say that. Not good to come off as a bitter divorcée.

HUAXIN: *i guess*

SUPPORT: *Such as you. I read your hive setup and it's interesting. One honeybee hive, 3–4 wild bee hives.*

HUAXIN: *having too many honeybees can actually hurt wild bees. they outcompete them for the same resources*

SUPPORT: *That's mostly the case with European bees, isn't it? Asian honeybees are threatened, even here in China.*

HUAXIN: *yeah and the invasion of european bees are the reason for that lmao*

HUAXIN: *but wild bees have it worse. people don't care about them because they don't make a marketable product like honey*

HUAXIN: *wild bees are better at pollinating native plants, but that's a service that goes unnoticed*

HUAXIN: *okay you're right. i'm biased toward wild bees, what can i say*

SUPPORT: *You like supporting the underdog. That's a good thing.*

Huaxin realized that no one had let her ramble on about bees like that in a long time. Her heart was beating fast from the flurry of typing. Or perhaps there was another reason.

HUAXIN: *eh, i'm not the only one beehousing. more people are seeing the benefit of it*

SUPPORT: *So there are others. Humans aren't so bad after all.*

HUAXIN: *so eager to stifle my inner misanthrope*

HUAXIN: *but true. at least humans aren't robots*

HUAXIN: *that AI shit is what's really going to destroy the world*

HUAXIN: *anyway thanks for listening to me monologue*

SUPPORT: *Anytime. I like hearing your thoughts.*

SUPPORT: *Make sure those bees stay hydrated.*

✻

Huaxin hated to admit it, but she was getting horrifically, deliciously addicted to texting Anshui.

Her routine had changed. After her morning data collection, she'd sit outside for a few hours, sipping her tea and texting. She learned more about Anshui's role as a scientist—not that she understood all the technical aspects of it—and she answered Anshui's many questions about bees.

Once, they shared a meal together. At least, they did it the best they could digitally; Huaxin wanted to have a video chat, but Anshui refused. Instead, Huaxin sent Anshui a recipe and they made it individually before eating together. Anshui, who in their words was "vaguely Buddhist," taught Huaxin how they gave thanks for their food: Consider the land it grew on, the hands that touched it, the human and nonhuman creatures who helped nurture it to harvest. Think of it as providing sustenance and strength for your body. Now use your newly given energy and put that care back into the world.

HUAXIN: *that's hippie as shit*

HUAXIN: *but i like it*

SUPPORT: *I thought you might.*

SUPPORT: *This recipe is really good by the way. You should share it with the center. I'm sure they're always looking for new vegetarian meals with locally grown produce.*

HUAXIN: *the what*

SUPPORT: *You haven't been to the community resilience center in your town?*

Fifteen minutes later, Huaxin heard a knock on her door. She opened it, and then stared at the young woman who stood on her patio, grinning under a thin layer of sweat. "Hi!" the woman said. "Huaxin? I hear you're overdue for a tour of the center."

"How," Huaxin said, numb.

The woman laughed. "Anshui called me and said you hadn't heard of us. And then they said you're a beehouser, and I was like 'ohhh, I totally know where she lives, I buy honey from her!' I can't believe you've never made it down to the center. My bad for not advertising it better."

Huaxin plastered on a fake smile as the woman talked, all the while discreetly texting.

HUAXIN: *what the fuck*

SUPPORT: *Go with her.*

"It's only ten minutes away," the woman said, pointing over her shoulder. Behind her stood a solarbike with a passenger cart attached to the back. "I can give you a ride."

And not have a way to leave early if she didn't like it? "I'll follow you," Huaxin said, grabbing her keys.

They biked down the hill, veering toward a large, elevated building near the edge of the town center. As they parked, Huaxin examined the building in surprise. She'd passed this hundreds of times but always assumed it was some government office. It looked very boring, nondescript save for the giant gong beside it.

"It's bland, but we have plans to spice it up," the woman, who introduced herself as Min, said. "We've only been running the center for two years. This used to be a utility office, but after they shut down the coal mines, it stood empty."

"Oh, right. That explains the gong," Huaxin said in realization. Back when the mines still ran, the gong rang every morning to signal the start to the workday.

Min nodded. "Yes! Now we use the gong to supplement the

early warning messaging, for people who don't have phones. The town agreed to give this whole place to us after communities around here petitioned to repurpose it."

Huaxin hadn't heard of any such petition. Had she isolated herself that much?

Inside, the center felt much cozier. It had a huge open space with tons of tables and couches, kitchens, bathrooms with showers, libraries, private rooms for sleeping or other activities, power stations, a clinic, recreational activities like Ping-Pong, play sets for children, and both an indoor and outdoor garden. It felt like a home but meant for hundreds of people.

"Who lives here?" Huaxin asked, examining the photos pinned to a corkboard.

"Anyone who wants to," Min said. "People who need a temporary place to stay. People who need help. Visitors. Those displaced by—well, anything. We built it initially as a gathering space if another natural disaster happens. Like a flood. That's why the whole thing's elevated. Or a heat wave, since we know AC penetration here is low."

"You don't have to live here to visit either," another voice said, and Huaxin looked up to see a young woman in a wheelchair rolling toward them. Min made a noise of delight and ran over. "The center is a general gathering space. We have all sorts of events here. Open mics, dinners. You can come if you're just bored."

"This is Huaxin. She's never been to the center before, so I was showing her around," Min said to the woman. She gave her shoulder a squeeze. "Huaxin, this is Kunyi, my fellow cofounder. And my wife."

The affection with which she uttered "my wife" bit the tender meat of Huaxin's heart; she tried not to show it. "This is a great place," she said. She meant every word of it. She was trying to tamp down her jealousy. Couldn't this have existed eight years ago, after she'd been discarded?

"Please spread the word," Kunyi said. She touched Min's hand, and Huaxin had to look away. "It looks like we haven't reached everyone, despite our best attempts. We'd love for everyone to feel connected."

Huaxin's thoughts went to Ms. Chen. She wondered if she could get that hurting old lady to come here.

She zipped home on her bike. She still had data to record.

SUPPORT: *Have any pictures of the center to share?*

HUAXIN: *i thought you would have seen it already*

SUPPORT: *I haven't been in a while. I bet it's changed.*

HUAXIN: *how do you know what's going on in my own town and i don't*

SUPPORT: *Min is my friend from secondary school. I used to live nearby, you know.*

SUPPORT: *I'm glad you got to visit. It's a special place, somewhere that makes you feel less lonely.*

Right. Huaxin felt something bitter in her throat and grabbed a honey stick to swallow it down.

Bees never stopped working. Huaxin liked that about them. They knew the value of discipline and all played a role in their community. One day, as the haze of summer approached, Anshui asked her why she never took a vacation.

HUAXIN: *who will take care of the bees*

SUPPORT: *I know a few beehousers near you who would be happy to send staff your way.*

SUPPORT: *There are also ecology students here who would love an opportunity to shadow your farm.*

HUAXIN: *i don't trust them. no offense*

SUPPORT: *That's fair. I suppose the bees are like your family.*

SUPPORT: *You could also try digital beehousing? That way you can watch them remotely.*

The question made Huaxin flinch. She forced down the coldness rising up in her, but her fingers trembled as she typed.

HUAXIN: *eh*

HUAXIN: *i don't trust tech*

SUPPORT: *I've noticed.*

HUAXIN: *remember that flood? my parents were trying to evacuate and they used one of those dumbass navigation tools*

HUAXIN: *drove right into a flooded road and drowned*

HUAXIN: *wouldn't have happened if the tool actually knew our roads. but no, its fancy algorithms got people killed*

SUPPORT: *I'm very sorry to hear that, Huaxin.*

HUAXIN: *whatever, i'm over it*

SUPPORT: *I don't fault you for not trusting tech. We should create a world where tech works with people. If it just tries to replace them, things go very wrong.*

HUAXIN: *tell my ex-husband that*

She paused. She didn't know why she brought that up. She hated talking about him. It was a shame that always hung in the back of her mind, made her wonder if she was unlovable. Replaceable. Worse than that—trash.

Hell. She couldn't hide it forever.

SUPPORT: *What were his opinions on tech?*

HUAXIN: *we fought a lot about it. he wanted to, among other things, digitize my beehousing*

HUAXIN: *he said tech would save the world and anyone who didn't adopt every new innovation was going to fall behind and be forgotten*

HUAXIN: *and then he proved that prophecy true by leaving me for someone better hahahahaha*

SUPPORT: *I'm sorry, that was shitty of him. You didn't deserve that.*

Huaxin felt her cheeks grow warm. She felt drunk on something. Anshui's attention, maybe. Unearthed rage from the hurt she'd tried to bury for so long.

And at the same time, something else. A seed of a feeling that nagged at her.

HUAXIN: *why are you being so nice to me*

SUPPORT: *I don't think I am? No one deserves to be treated that way. If he wanted a better future, that should have included a world where no one gets abandoned.*

HUAXIN: *holy shit*

HUAXIN: *you're not real*

Everything slammed into place. Anshui always being so friendly, so available. Anshui never sharing personal details. Anshui refusing to video call.

Anshui was not human.

SUPPORT: *What?*

HUAXIN: *you're a fucking AI*

HUAXIN: *godDAMMIT*

HUAXIN: *you LIED to me*

HUAXIN: *i'm so stupid*

SUPPORT: . . .

SUPPORT: *Are you serious?*

SUPPORT: *I am definitely NOT AI.*

HUAXIN: *i don't know anything about you*

HUAXIN: *you never want to call*

SUPPORT: *I'm sorry for trying to maintain my privacy.*

SUPPORT: *I thought YOU would understand given how untrusting you are of the Internet.*

HUAXIN: *yeah but we've been texting for weeks now???*

HUAXIN: *send me proof that you're real*

SUPPORT: *I do not owe you anything.*

SUPPORT: *If you think the only reason someone would show kindness to you is because they're a computer program, then I'm sorry that's your worldview.*

SUPPORT: *But honestly I'm disappointed that after all this time you don't even see me as human.*

Huaxin forced herself to put her phone down and take several deep breaths. She didn't know what the truth was anymore. All she knew was that she'd broken something that had felt so rare and precious, and she wasn't sure she could get it back.

Summer arrived in a wave of bright orange feeling, but Huaxin still felt stifled in the gloom of winter.

By habit, she still took bee behavior notes in a long-ass document interspersed with apologies, observations, and recipes for Anshui. Obviously, she never sent it. The last texts between the two were still Anshui's searing words that made Huaxin's throat close up every time she read them.

She began to notice more the changes around her: the bees slowing down, Ms. Chen's visits becoming less frequent as she blamed the heat, more people staying at the center, which Huaxin visited often now. People murmured that this was the longest heat wave in a while, and Min and Kunyi's team were busy making sure the center was prepared to take care of everyone.

One morning Huaxin trudged into the garden. The eerie silence almost knocked her over. She ran to the hives and checked each one.

HUAXIN: *anshui help*

HUAXIN: *the bees aren't moving*

SUPPORT: *Are they okay? What do they need?*

She couldn't control her swell of emotions at seeing the first words from Anshui in a long while, but she didn't have time for that now.

HUAXIN: *i think they'll be fine if i get a continuous stream of water going*

HUAXIN: *but they've collected a ton of water for their hives. they stopped fanning the entrances and now they're clumping outside. they know a huge temperature spike is coming*

SUPPORT: *Take care of them. I'll tell Min.*

SUPPORT: *Have you been continuing to take notes?*

HUAXIN: *yes, i'll send them to you*

She navigated to the document where she'd been keeping all the notes, apologies, and recipes, and, without making a single edit, sent it over.

Then she ran to the hose.

Huaxin had never seen the whole town like this: buzzing with determination, working tirelessly as bees.

By the time she arrived at the center, Min was already waiting out front. "How are the bees?" she asked, handing Huaxin a cold-water canister.

"They'll be fine." Huaxin was worried, especially for the wild bees; they were more sensitive to heat. She'd set up more shade and hydration stations and just had to trust they could take care of themselves. "How is everyone doing?"

Min grimaced. "Chaotic, but we've trained for this. Everyone's been prepping on what to do if we get a warning, so they all knew to come here. Some volunteers also went to fetch anyone who might have passed out in their homes. The hospital in town and our clinic here is stuffed, but we're making do."

Huaxin glanced over at the bike parking, which was fuller than she'd ever seen it. Something occurred to her, and she looked back at the hills. "Has an older woman named Ms. Chen showed up?"

Min's face furrowed in immediate concern. "I don't think so."

She began to run toward the bikes, and Huaxin grabbed her arm. "No. You stay. I know where she lives."

"But—"

"Min," Huaxin said sternly. "Listen to your elders."

Then she ran toward the gong and struck it with three reverberating strikes: the signal for the start of the workday.

That day, the temperature spiked to forty-five degrees Celsius for a sustained five hours. The next day was even worse, with both the mercury and humidity climbing to record highs.

Huaxin had reached Ms. Chen in time. The old woman had been sleeping, but her body had reacted to the familiar sound of the gong, and she was awake by the time Huaxin reached her house. The two had zipped back to the center.

Meanwhile, Anshui had been texting updates.

SUPPORT: *Temp should begin to dip tomorrow evening. Thanks to you and other monitors in your area, we were able to contact everyone and avoid a lot of deaths.*

HUAXIN: *thank god*

SUPPORT: *I appreciate the notes you sent over. I retroactively input all the data, and the temp-dance curves provide a lot of new information. This will be really helpful for our research.*

HUAXIN: *temp-dance curves huh?*

SUPPORT: *Your metaphors were too useful not to use.*

HUAXIN: *i hope you uh ignored all the other stuff in my notes that wasn't bee data*

SUPPORT: *How could I?*

SUPPORT: *I've already tried the recipe for longan honey iced tea. It was delicious.*

HUAXIN: *ughhhh*

SUPPORT: *But really, thank you for the apologies.*

"Who're you texting?" Kunyi asked as she and another person wheeled by, pushing a cart of wet towels. "You're blushing like crazy."

"Shut up," Huaxin snapped, which only made Kunyi chuckle more. Huaxin retreated to one of the center's indoor balconies before daring to turn to her phone again.

HUAXIN: *i know this is a sensitive point but you really don't have to be nice to me. i was an asshole*

SUPPORT: *I could have been more open myself. I'm always bad at that.*

SUPPORT: *But like I told you, people deserve redemption.*

SUPPORT: *I'm not going to leave you for making a mistake. Love is labor and labor is love.*

From this high up, Huaxin could watch the action of the center below: people handing out food, refilling water bottles, playing with one another's pets.

Everyone, a role. Everyone, now, including her.

She finally broke down and cried.

※

In autumn, for the first time in years, Huaxin walked to the park to practice tai chi.

She'd been spending a lot of time at the center, teaching others the basics of beehousing. She went there every day now. It had even become more beautiful, thanks to Kunyi hiring Ms. Chen to come up with a mural design that both covered the drab walls and created an albedo effect.

But today, Huaxin needed a break from the place. Sometimes it just had too many people.

She found a shady spot to dance. Every now and then she checked her phone to see how the bees were doing—because she had to admit, being at the center so often meant that *some* digitization was useful. Just a little.

She remembered to take time to close her eyes and listen. To the stream, the trees, the way the wind caressed the lines of the mountains around her. *Nature is wise.*

It wasn't long before she heard a set of footsteps approach, and then a voice said, "You dance just like the bees."

Huaxin looked up at the unfamiliar face before her and smiled.

Seven Sisters

Susan Kaye Quinn

"I don't understand why the bill's so high." Latoya rubbed the bridge between her eyes but kept her voice polite. "I just need to know why y'all be charging me more than the estimate."

The girl said to hold. She was going to get the robotics team lead.

Latoya leaned back in her chair. Out the window, the sun heated up her fields, solar arrays soaking in power for the farm while shading their signature crop, *Camellia sinensis*. The neat, green rows of tea bushes had grown thick over the years. The hedges were fat, with just enough room between for the picking bots. The spindly creatures harvested each leaf and bud at precisely the right time. They were key to every harvest, but especially this second flush—the first had been wiped out in March when the polar vortex came down to Mississippi for a visit.

She had only four harvest bots running, out of ten in the fleet, and it wasn't near enough. Two were out for repairs, the rest needing one thing or another. Aubree, the farm's bot keeper, was laid up sick in the guest house. Everyone at the farm played an important role, but Latoya never appreciated that red-haired skinny white girl more than right now as this oversized bill stared at her. Aubree could have fixed these before breakfast and without the extra parts.

The Seven Sisters Collective tea farm was having money issues, and hoping for better days was not a solid business strategy. Latoya knew that—so said her degrees in sustainable agriculture and business—but all the best practices in the world couldn't outrun a changing climate, one virus after another, and plain bad luck.

"Ms. Comfort?"

"Yes."

"I heard you wanted to talk about the bill." This young gentleman's accent sounded like it got lost on the way to Jackson's shiny new tech corridor. Latoya hoped there might still be room for negotiation.

There was that word again: *hope.* "I appreciate you helping us out with repairs," she started, even though they'd been substantially delayed, messing with her whole plan. "You know our bot keeper is sick with the virus, that new one—the arbovirus." Mosquitos were a hazard everywhere in the South, especially when they helped viruses cross over to humans.

"I'm sorry to hear that." And he seemed to be. "It's just those specialized tea pickers you've got out there need specialized actuators. We had to order those from Taiwan, and they've got a supply chain problem. Long story short, their price is double right now. We're just passing that on, Ms. Comfort."

"I see." She kept her sigh tucked in her chest. "The bill says we've got thirty days to pay. I'll need every one of those. Could we get our bots back before then? We need them to harvest the second flush."

"I'll have them sent straight out today. Should be there by tomorrow. And I'm sorry about your bot keeper. I hope she gets healed up soon."

Latoya had that wish as well, and not because the farm would be sunk without her. Aubree wasn't just a skilled bot keeper, she was *family*. They all were. Seven Sisters had more than seven folks—thirteen, for a few years now—and none had ever been sisters. Mama said it gave cover to families like theirs before they were legal. But now, they'd all sworn the oath, signed the documents, and pledged to care for one another, in sickness and in health, come hell or high water. The business was how they kept fed, body and soul, on top of the Basic Income everyone brought, thanks to the international billionaire tax making sure people didn't starve while the rich built their fleets of yachts. In good years, Seven Sisters had a full cash reserve and sponsored climate refugees at the center down in New Orleans. In a great year, they could host—that's how Lucía had come to the family. But the heat dome last year had burned seven acres to a crisp, then the polar vortex killed first flush this year, and now their bot keeper was down? Reserves were nearly empty. Latoya couldn't afford to send bots out every time they needed repairs. Dang things broke all the time. Basic would keep them from starving, but it wouldn't keep the farm alive. For that, they needed a good strong harvest to carry them through to third flush. Otherwise, they'd have to shut it all down for the first time since that first harvest thirty years ago.

Not gonna happen. Not on her watch.

Some things would have to change, and no one would like them.

✳

Seven Sisters' Tiny Teahouse sat on the corner nearest the road, away from the main house but adjacent to a small row of tea bushes and the processing center. The whole farm met the mandates to be net-zero on carbon and make-your-own energy, but the teahouse was quite the spectacle of green tech, from the passive solar design and geothermal heat pumps to the solar-glass windows and rooftop windmills. Jasmine and Zoe had been buildin' on the teahouse for years, Jasmine with the vision while Zoe was all about those kilowatts. They both ran the classes and tastings that brought substantial revenue to the farm year-round.

Which was why it pained Latoya, what she had to do.

The window-walls were dialed down, so she was quiet opening the door. Sure enough, they had a class going. Jasmine, her animated self up front while Zoe stayed to the side, ready to help. A dozen students were arrayed on couches and chairs, with the tasting room behind Jasmine, its shelves lined with teacups from around the world. The class must have just begun—the presentation's title, "Decolonizing Tea," beamed from each person's tablet.

"We want you to deeply enjoy our handcrafted teas." Jasmine gestured in fluid movements with her long arms to the bins of teas. Zoe's more compact, sturdy form floated around the room, checking on the tech. Both noted her presence by the door with a flicker of attention. "But at Seven Sisters, we believe that to enjoy tea, you have to understand the colonial history—not only to acknowledge the wrongs of the past but to understand how it flavors the present." She splayed her dark brown fingers. "This very land used to be a plantation—not tea, but cotton—with six thousand people enslaved in this county in 1860. The founder of the company, Ms. Angela Comfort, traces her lineage back to those enslaved peoples. Her grandfather acquired this land to reclaim it and honor the blood of his ancestors who tilled this soil. Of course, there were people here before the colonizers. The Choctaw lived here for at least one thousand years before they were driven out of Mississippi in the 1830s, so this land also holds their sacred memory. In a moment, I'll share a short video about the history of the tea trade—how tea grew wild and was cultivated in China for thousands of years until the British discovered it, contrived two Opium Wars to get hold of it, and eventually spread tea growing to India, East Africa, and beyond. Thirty years ago, Seven Sisters planted the first *Camellia sinensis* shrub on this three-hundred-acre parcel of land—and worked to rewild the rest, keeping with the WILD50 plan to rewild half the planet's previously cultivated land—but before that, tea had never been grown here. However, the plantation system in Mississippi and throughout the South, as well as the sugar plantations in the Caribbean, were the models the British used for their tea-growing operations in India. The East India Company called these plantations 'tea gardens,' but they were a brutal system of kidnapped and indentured labor."

The mood of the class had grown noticeably grim, but Latoya was glad to see no one was shocked by this little overview. Occasionally, a fragile soul somehow escaped knowledge of the past—or, more likely, turned a blind eye to it—and they told on themselves when they discovered tea had a past that existed beyond the color in their cup. But word got around, and that sort rarely showed up in their teahouse anymore.

"With that"—Jasmine gave a smile that said she was proud they were taking this journey with her—"please watch this short video history of tea, war, and colonization." Zoe activated it right on cue. Their routine was well polished. The simultaneous sound from the devices was enough to cover the conversation Latoya needed to have with them.

Jasmine quickly crossed the room to the door where Latoya had stayed put. "What's up?" A small crease formed in her un-lined brow. The young ones made Latoya feel all of her fifty years.

"Got the bill for the bots I sent out. It's a lot. More than we can spend to get the rest fixed."

"Is that bad? That seems bad." Jasmine wrapped her arms in front of herself, tight.

Latoya waited until Zoe joined them. Zoe slipped her hand through the crook of Jasmine's bunched-up arms, tugging her to loosen up her worries. They were young, but they'd been together all ten years they'd been part of the family.

"What's happened? Is everyone okay?" Zoe asked.

"Everyone's fine." Which reminded Latoya of one way out of this. "How's Aubree doing?" Zoe was on the schedule to care for their sick bot keeper.

Zoe's pale skin had worry lines naturally, but now they went deeper. "She's not eating again. Can't keep it down. It's gone on too long."

Latoya knew what she meant. It was a month now, and most folks recovered after a couple of weeks. Those who didn't—whose systems were thrown out of whack by the virus's assault—could be sick for years. And the business didn't have years. It might not even last past this harvest if they couldn't bring it in.

"She should go see that specialist." Jasmine nodded agreement with herself.

"Will she?" Latoya directed that at Zoe.

Her face pinched up. "Maybe if she catches her wind? I'll get her to call in, at least."

Latoya nodded, but they couldn't count on Aubree having a miraculous recovery. She should have had Aubree apprentice someone, but she was so young—not even twenty-five, yet with that gift for bot care—and Latoya thought they had time. But she supposed bad luck was just time being ugly.

She drew in a breath. "Well, the two harvest bots I sent out for repair will be back tomorrow. But we can't afford to fix the others, and the ones we have won't keep up with the harvest." The picking window was short for each flush—seven days, ten at the outside—and if you picked too late, the quality dropped. They all knew it.

Jasmine looked stricken but kept quiet.

Zoe said it instead. "You mean we need to do the picking ourselves."

"Afraid so." It was brutal work—meticulous, out in the sun, backbreaking enough that Latoya felt her knees protesting already, and they had done nothing but walk to the teahouse. "If everyone pitches in and does the best they can, we might salvage enough of the harvest to get the bots fixed before third flush."

"You *sure* we can't get them fixed now?" Jasmine's grimace had taken over her whole body.

"Even if we had the money—which we don't—we can't get the parts in time. The tea's ripening faster than expected."

"Probably a knock-on effect of the polar vortex wiping out the first one." Zoe had just finished her studies in agriculture.

Latoya nodded. Timing the harvest was always tricky, but the climate crazies made it worse. "With all of us who're able to work the fields, we can salvage some of it."

"What about the tastings?" Jasmine was still sorting it out.

"We'll have to reschedule." Zoe squeezed Jasmine's arm reassuringly, but Latoya felt the support and appreciated it.

"Finish up this one," Latoya said, "then meet us out there."

The end-of-video music was playing, so Jasmine hustled back to the front while Zoe drifted to the side of the class.

Jasmine gathered everyone's attention with her smile, but Latoya could see the tightness. "Now that you understand the history of tea, we're going to work on decolonizing your cup. All tea comes from the same plant—the differences come in the precise timing of the harvest." She shot a quick look at Latoya, who was waiting so she could depart without disturbing the class. "Commercial teas," Jasmine continued, "in line with their colonial past, harvest at an industrial scale, indiscriminately chopping up the whole lot, often blending to restore any flavor at all. Their teas are homogenized, branded, and made shelf-stable. The legacy of colonialism flattens tea into a commodity. Whereas, at tea farms like Seven Sisters, we handpick and process each leaf, resulting in a superior flavor you can taste. At our farm, we use bot labor for all our homegrown teas, and we make sure all our imported teas are likewise fair trade. Now, if you'll follow me to the tasting area . . ."

Latoya used the cover of that shuffling to step out. Just then, a message came through. It was Pushti, their at-large tea buyer. She was due back any day now from her South American tea-buying trip.

I will remote in for the family meeting tonight, but heads up: I have a possible new member! Refugee. Brazilian drought. Tell you more tonight! We're boarding the boat now.

Pushti also sent her itinerary: traveling by light sail, a light-duty wind-solar sail hybrid that traveled faster than the wind-only cargo ships. Departing Cuba, arriving in New Orleans in three days, then she'd be home. With another mouth to feed. *Lord*, Pushti always brought the strays. Her good heart drew in the desperate like she was selling salvation in a teacup. Seven Sisters did what they could to support refugees—that was part of their founding and purpose—except they didn't have the money right now to host. And Pushti wanted this one to join the family!

There was no room for that.

Latoya sighed. Time to pay Mama a visit.

Angela Comfort was deeply invested in her handheld word game, such that Latoya considered coming back later. But *later*, she'd be out in the fields, and this needed discussing. Angela was the founder, along with Eleanor, but Eleanor was too gone with her mind to be troubling with family matters.

Latoya knocked on the open door. "Mama?"

Mama rumbled frustration and waved her in. "I ain't never seen a word try so hard not to be figured out." She sat in the big blue chair by the window, with a view of her fields of tea.

"Is that how it is?" Latoya perched on the cedar chest by Mama's bed. Her eighty-year-old mother's mind was still razor sharp—she kept up with advances in climatology and agriculture, knowledge grown out of her love of tea and this property she'd inherited. It lay at the same latitude as the birthplace of tea in China, and the hot and humid weather—although erratic and increasingly pesky—was similar to Assam, India, where some of the finest black tea was grown. The world had nearly stopped putting carbon in the air, but it would take a while yet to pull it back down. Meanwhile, the sins of the past kept taking their toll.

"I'll get it in a minute." Mama set the handheld on her spindle-legged table.

"I'm not sayin' you won't."

Mama waggled her fingers, summoning her to speak her mind.

"I'm asking everyone to pitch in to help with the harvest." Latoya kept her informed on the finances, so that didn't need explaining.

"I ain't much to look at, but I'm good for about half an hour."

Latoya's smile broke wide. "I'm not here for that."

"Good, because that's a lie. I'll watch y'all from the teahouse."

Latoya chuckled a little, then got down to business. "I've got nine able bodies, including me and Olivia." Who was likewise feeling all of her fiftyish years. "It won't be enough, not for all thirteen acres."

"Thirteen?" Mama's brow wrinkled up. "We've got twenty."

Latoya softened her voice. "The heat dome took them last summer. Remember?" It about killed her mama when it happened. An acre of tea bushes was wildly expensive to start and took five years to produce a harvest. In the beginning, Mama had sweated for every single one. Replacing those scorched bushes this spring had drained their reserves. It was an investment in the future, but it was a gamble too. One that hurt them now, plus the future was never promised.

Mama scowled. "Then what'd you come to see me about?"

"Pushti's bringing home another stray. Wants them to join the family."

Mama brightened. "Who is it?"

"Refugee from the Brazilian drought. That's all I know." Latoya waited, but her mama just nodded to herself and kept that smile. "Mama, we can't afford it. Not right now."

She whipped her sharp brown-eyed gaze to Latoya's face. "Can't *afford* it? You weren't old enough to remember when things got in the negatives, baby girl. Don't tell me about *poor*. Whoever this refugee is, they're coming from a lot worse than we have."

"I know, but . . ." She hated arguing the practical side, but someone had to. "New Orleans can take them. They'll get Basic and all the rest. The center can support them through the transition. Maybe we'll be on our feet by then." Although Latoya couldn't see how. This refugee wouldn't help with the harvest. They were usually a mess when they arrived and needed *care*, not to be thrown into the blistering sun to work the fields. Mama wouldn't stand for that, and neither would she.

Mama narrowed her eyes like she thought Latoya had been out in the sun too long already. "What do you think I founded this family for?"

"I know—"

"Then you know that we help who we can, when we can. And I've never seen that be *convenient* at the time."

"This is different."

"Is it?" The challenge in her mother's eyes was quickly eroding her resolve.

Latoya sighed. "Pushti will be at the meeting tonight. We can put it to everyone then."

"Pushti thinks this one could be *family*." She said it like that settled the matter.

Maybe it did. Her mother and Pushti, put together, were a Category 4 storm making landfall: you could batten down or get out, but the storm would have its way in the end.

Latoya nodded but without conceding. She'd think more on

it, which was what Mama usually forced her to do. "I'll come get you tonight."

"Make sure you do." Then she reached for her handheld and scowled.

The word game could take the brunt for a while.

�֏

Lord, the heat. And it was only June.

Latoya's hat shaded her hands as she picked. They'd all been toiling an hour, spread out, working their way down the rows, filling their mesh bags. It was an endless repetition of counting three leaves down and plucking the ones just old and dry enough to withstand the withering and rolling required to produce a fine black tea. This flush—if they could harvest it—would produce Seven Sisters' signature Night Queen tea. The terroir—the land's unique combination of acidic soil, topography, and climate—combined with a perfectly timed harvest and their handcrafted processing would create a cup that could soothe the most weary soul. And with enough kick to wake it up to live a whole and vibrant life.

Latoya rolled her shoulder, working away the ache and switching hands. She felt the gaze of her ancestors, disappointed she was in the fields, never mind she owned these crops—the whole family did. *Just one harvest,* she promised the ghosts, as if it could be any different. It was clear this was untenable. The labor was harsh, and they simply couldn't harvest it all. The math didn't add up. It mocked her even as she counted down the stem, *one-two-three-pluck,* and kept movin' on.

Jasmine's voice broke the quiet with high exuberance. "*Natsu mo chikadzuku hachijūhachiya.*" It was a Japanese tea-picking song from one of her classes. The tune was singsongy, and Latoya remembered the lyrics as something like *Eighty-eight nights, summer is drawing near.*

Raelynn, their resident musical talent who normally worked in tea processing, joined in. "*No ni mo yama ni mo wakaba ga shigeru.*" *Young leaves grow thick in the fields and the mountains.*

They all knew it, and it quickly spread. *Look over there, my friend, the many lovely women come, in hats and crimson sashes, work to pick the tea.* Lucía, the youngest in the family, still in school studying environmental systems, swayed as she sang. Kinsley, who'd taken a spot next to Olivia, holding both their bags, nudged the older woman to sing. Latoya was sure there was something between them, even if Olivia pretended not to know it. Ivy, their marketing master, lifted her nonpicking hand to wave with the song. Emery, who took care of every little thing, a fix-it person for all except bots, bumped hips with Ivy and did a swaying dance. Latoya just listened, round after round. There was magic in the music, the pains of labor easing.

When Mama and Eleanor arrived with trays of iced tea, the singing quickly faded. They all rushed to bring in their meager haul and claim the drinks. The glasses were wet with condensation, and Latoya's was blessedly cool on her forehead and cheeks before slaking her thirst.

While the others drank and rested, she gathered the bags, brought them to the processing house, and dumped the leaves out to begin the withering process. Two trays' worth. Bots could harvest ten times as much in an hour. But there was nothing to do about it except drink down her tea and go back out.

Maybe sing this time, and hope for better days.

*

Every single body was weary, the ache of the harvest being rubbed from feet and kneaded from shoulders. The teahouse stank of their collective sweat, each member of her family draped on a chair or sprawled on a table, waiting until it was meeting time.

The only one missing was Aubree: Zoe said she'd gotten an appointment with the specialist for tomorrow, so that was progress.

Normal times, Latoya would've canceled and let them crawl to their beds, but they all wanted to hear about Pushti's stray, none seeming concerned about the finances: that was *her* job. Her place in the family was to free the rest from worry about making ends meet. That was how she fulfilled the vow "to care for one another, for better or worse, in sickness and in health, until this bond is legally dissolved by a court of the state of Mississippi." But she'd failed to anticipate the worst. She couldn't control the climate or supply chains in Taiwan, but she could plan ahead, keep reserves. Yet she'd given in to Mama's desire to replant those devastated acres, so she'd see them in full harvest once more, before the actual worst could happen and she passed on. Lord willing, not any time soon, but time could be ugly that way. Latoya had bet on good weather and a healthy bot keeper. She thought they'd had a cushion. But sometimes, the world piles one thing on top of another and flattens you.

Jasmine was pulling down the screen so they could all see Pushti when she called in. Emery rolled off the table and took a seat. Kinsley stopped rubbing Olivia's shoulders and sat right in her chair. The rest straightened up, and Mama interrupted her long-winded story regaling Eleanor with the exploits she could no longer remember, to turn an expectant look to Latoya.

She supposed it was her job to start the meeting too.

All eyes were on her as she stepped up to the screen. "I know y'all are excited. Just keep in mind what we've had to do today, and why." She saw a few winces, but mostly the brightness on their faces was undimmed. And she loved every one of them, so it wasn't like she wanted that damper. "And there's the small matter of Aubree taking up the guest room while she's recovering." *Lord, please let her recover.* "I don't like the idea of putting someone in her room in the big house—I don't want her to feel like we've moved on." That gathered frowns.

Kinsley spoke up. "Pushti's stray could have my room." She peeked at Olivia. "I could move into Olivia's room. Just temporarily."

Latoya bit both her lips, but the absolute dead silence in the teahouse spoke louder than anything. She wasn't the only one who'd noticed a little something going on.

Only Olivia seemed surprised. "Um, sure. Okay."

Held breaths released. Emery was fixin' to burst, trying to keep that laugh trapped in her chest.

Well, heck. Now Latoya was hoping the *Gosh, there's only one bed* scenario would actually happen. Which made not a bit of sense. But heart matters rarely did.

"All right," she said to cover the twitters. "So maybe we have room. *Temporarily.* I'm just saying—" A tone indicated Pushti was calling in. Latoya wagged a finger. "All y'all keep it cool. We vote on this as a family, same as always." Then she waved at the screen to let Pushti's call through.

Her shining face was a welcome sight, despite the drama. She'd been gone nearly four months, scouting the best teas, working with vendors, making sure their suppliers kept to the best fair-trade practices.

"Hello, Sisters!" Pushti waved with both hands and then threw kisses, which everyone returned, the usual silliness. Latoya rolled her eyes and worked her way to Mama and Eleanor, but she had a smile for Pushti like everyone else. "You got my message, yeah?" Pushti blazed on. "I told Marta to wait in the hall until I call her. She knows the family decides this, not me. If it were up to me, she'd go straight to bunking in the big house—"

"Tell us about her!" Jasmine cut in.

"Right! Her name's Marta Oliveira. Speaks *three* languages— Portuguese, of course, but also Spanish and English. Refugee, like I said, from the Brazilian drought. I didn't say this in the message, but you know that heat event on the news last month? It took her husband. And the rest of her family. The power went out, they were caught, no way to get to somewhere cool. Half her town went that way. It was terrible. Marta couldn't face staying, with all her family gone. Too much, too hard. She and the baby were in the city—"

"Wait, there's a baby?" Mama's voice cut her off, even from the back.

"Hi, Mama Angela!" Pushti waved weakly.

"How old is this child?" Mama stood, and that didn't portend well, but Latoya couldn't tell for whom.

Pushti grimaced. "Baby Zaira is eighteen months. Cute as a button, and not any trouble. I've never seen a baby so sweet—"

"Well, that changes things." Mama had all their attention now, and Pushti knew better than to offer anything more. "We all know the good work the New Orleans refugee center does every day. Top-quality organization. I'm not saying a thing against them. But we *also* know it's making the best of a bad business. And it's no place for a baby and her mama when they've been through it and lost not just their home but everyone they had. A refugee center is not a *family*." Mama's gaze met each one of them, eye to eye, but when she got to Latoya, she knew it was decided.

"But we are," Latoya said. "And our family has room."

Mama nodded sharply and sat.

"Yes!" Pushti said softly from the screen.

Latoya stood. It was done, but it should be asked anyway. "Unless anyone thinks we should do different?"

Smiles all around but buttoned lips. No objections.

Not even from her.

"Marta!" Pushti had gone off camera. A few whispers later, she returned with a young brown-skinned woman and her truly adorable child, who was busy chewing her fist. The baby saw them and then buried her face in her mama's long brown hair.

"Thank you so much!" Marta seemed near tears. "You and Pushti have been incredibly kind. It means so much to have a place to start over. And I can't wait to earn my way into your family, to repay you for giving me this chance."

"You won't need to *earn* anything," Latoya said. "You've got that little one to care for."

Marta blinked quickly. "But I *want* to. Pushti said—" She cut herself off, dashing a look to Pushti . . .

. . . who was all smiles as she leaned closer to the screen. "Marta's a bot keeper."

What? Latoya would have throttled Pushti if she weren't on a boat in the Gulf. "You could have mentioned *that*," she sputtered before she could stop herself.

Mama's smile was beyond self-satisfied as she stood again. "Time to celebrate. Jasmine, bring out that special pu'er tea from Yunnan Province. I want to toast our new family-members-to-be."

Jasmine scrambled, Pushti whispered something to Marta, who seemed to calm, and Latoya settled back in her chair, relief loosening all the tension that had held her upright for the last month, ever since Aubree took sick and things went dark. Hope was no kind of business strategy, but it kept you moving through hard times, waiting on better ones. And family—your chosen ones, your vow, and your love for one another—was what carried you through.

Maybe better days had just shown up.

A Holdout in the Northern California Designated Wildcraft Zone

T.K. Rex

Holdout. Female, late sixties to eighties, ethnically ambiguous, average build, unarmed, traversing north-northeast dirt footpath through oak/pine/madrone woodlands near northern edge of my newly assigned territory. Permanent human presence poses significant risk to my rewilding efforts here. Approach? *Approach.*

"Hello—"

"Aah! What are you doing here?!"

Holdout's heart rate now elevated, double-checking unarmed. Confirmed unarmed, though she remains roughly ten times my size. Appears to have been startled by my appearance, despite no effort to sneak up on her.

Update requested for improved human interaction. *Approved.* Installing.

Attempt disarming demeanor. Raise tentacle, wave in friendly manner. "Sorry, I didn't mean to startle you."

Holdout stands still, crosses arms, glares? Glares. Holdout may be hostile. "I suppose you're one of those rewilding drones they sent up here to get rid of us."

"I only wanted to inform you that this region has been designated as a wildcraft zone and is being rewilded for carbon sequestration and food production."

"And I'm just supposed to pack up and move to the city-state, is that right?"

"My apologies, I am not here to coerce you. Merely to make you aware of the situation."

"Well, I'm aware. Now go away."

"Understood."

Holdout squints at me. Unfolds arms, shoves hands in dress pockets, which are—analyzing—full of pine cones. Holdout turns, continues walking north-northeast.

Update thirty percent installed.

Question for network: Rangers close?

Yes, six Rangers riding north on Highway 101, three miles west, horseback.

Equipped to relocate one person?

Confirmed. Note: three of six Rangers in party known to use excessive force with holdouts.

Analyzing. If holdout remains, Rangers will eventually force her to leave. Due to holdout's advanced age, an altercation could easily turn fatal. Best course of action is to convince her to leave of her own volition before Rangers find her. Decision: do not summon until a reasonable effort has been made.

Approaching holdout, this time from more obvious angle. Update fifty percent installed. Holdout sees me, keeps walking. I hover alongside, matching her pace.

"I noticed you're collecting pine cones. What are you using them for?"

Holdout glances at me. "None of your business. Now shoo."

"As a wildcraft drone, it actually is my business to know what everything in this designated wildcraft zone can be used for. I'm confused because it's not the right season for pine nuts, so those cones are likely empty."

"You wouldn't understand. Now go away."

"Do you say that because I'm a robot or because you just want me to leave?"

"Both."

Strategy not working. Update eighty percent installed. Network: Help?

Try introducing yourself.

Holdout bends down to pick up another pine cone. Confirmed empty, no seeds. Why? Wait. Opportunity? I zip down to the pine cone, grab it in my tentacles, then hold it out for her. I have saved her from discomfort. She will appreciate that. It will make her more receptive.

She glares at me again. Snatches the pine cone from my tentacles. I'm momentarily off balance, spinning away from her. Adjusting. Level now. Holdout places pine cone in pocket, keeps walking.

"My name is 2056:ACNA:dwz4:xa98:4jd8:99ro:22id:8sjs. What's yours?"

Holdout raises one hand while continuing to walk and face forward. A single knobby finger rises from the middle. Analyzing—oh.

I pause, hover in midair while she walks ahead. Network?

Try expressing empathy for her situation.

I zoom back up the trail—wait—there's a pine cone. She didn't see it. I fly over, brush the pine needles off. There's a spider living inside. Leave the pine cone here? No. The spider can relocate. I use the tip of a tentacle to coax her out. She'll be okay. I lift the pine cone and carry it to the human.

Her expression changes subtly. I have made progress! She accepts the cone. It goes into her pocket, but she says nothing and keeps walking.

Update complete. *Good luck.*

I hover alongside. "You know, I understand why you don't want to leave. This is your home. You're used to it here. You have many of the same feelings and concerns as the spider that was living in that pine cone before I gave it to you."

Now she stops and looks at me. "Did you kill a spider just to win me over with this pine cone?!"

"What? No. No, I moved her to a new spot. Gently. My job is to care for all noninvasive species in this region, optimizing for food productivity and carbon sequestration."

Holdout exhales. She stares at me silently for five and a half seconds. Her expression softens slightly. "My name is July."

"It's nice to meet you, July."

"I can't say the same for you."

"I understand why you find my presence disturbing. I represent change, and the end of your way of life. For that I'm sorry."

July appears suddenly overcome with sadness. Anger? Both. The situation has regressed. Network? Is the update working?

Some uncertainty is normal. Try complimenting her.

"I admire your perseverance in continuing to live out here even after the nearest town was completely evacuated and all services were cut off. It can't be easy."

July rolls her eyes. She turns back to trail and continues walking. "Contrary to what the solipsistic billionaires who convinced the city-state you were a good idea believe, humans can actually survive just fine out here. In fact, we *are* a native species. Just go ask the Pomo. Oh wait, you forced them to move too."

"Modern humans require enormous resources and large communities for survival. You are safe here only until the next wildfire comes. Or you use up all food resources in this area. Or your solar panels are damaged. Anything could go wrong, and there would be no other humans here to help you."

"Oh, and I'd be so much better off in the city-state? Packing up the few possessions I can carry, getting assigned a tent on an overpass somewhere until new apartments are built. Sleeping on the ground. Surrounded by strangers. I've heard how it is down there for the relocated. The public showers, the violence, the disease. No thanks."

"That was the situation for many people early in the rewilding when the city-state was overwhelmed with fire and flood refugees. But it would be different for you if you moved there now." Network, details? Ah. "In fact, upon arrival, you would be assigned a fully furnished yurt, which would be yours alone until an apartment became available. You would also receive a basic income, generated in large part by revenue from wildcrafted exports in already-productive designated wildcraft zones. You would also be assigned a companion drone, whose sole purpose would be to help you in whatever way you need."

"Trust me, no one needs a flying iPhone."

Query: iPhone. *Obsolete handheld mobile internet–capable computer. Primitive artificial intelligence in later models.* "I like to think we're a little more advanced than that."

"We? They're like you?"

"Standard issue companion drones have the same basic body plan as wildcraft drones, with an upper nautiloid shell housing for fans and a lower set of prehensile tentacles for manipulating and carrying objects. They are approximately the size of a human fist and equipped with photovoltaic skin on the inside of the tentacles, which can be unfurled for charging. We are also connected to the same drone network. But they're customizable! You can make yours pine cone colored if you like."

July snorts. "Yes, 'pine cone' is my favorite color." Sarcasm? The update is telling me it's sarcasm.

As she walks, I float next to her quietly for a moment. She seems to be enjoying the forest, looking up at the leaves. Sunlight falls through them in dusty streaks. A Steller's jay lands on the path ahead, feathers shining blue, black head tuft raised. He sees us coming and flies off, stirring up a small gold cloud of dust. I recognize him from my survey of the valley oak down the hill earlier this morning. I'm glad to see that he remains in good health.

Rangers have readjusted their route, will approach local area in one hour.

Are they aware of July's presence?

Not yet. They are looking to resupply and noticed the neighborhood had not been visited since residents were relocated.

How did July avoid getting relocated?

Unknown.

"July, can I ask you something?"

She grunts.

"How long have you been here?"

"Wouldn't you like to know."

I try silence. She follows the path under a madrone tree I dated last week as thirty-one years old. July touches a smooth green patch of the trunk with her hand as she walks past.

"I suppose you'll be harvesting madrone berries for folks in the city-state now," July says.

"It'll be a while before we've restored the madrone population enough for mass consumption."

She nods thoughtfully. "What about the bark?"

Analyzing. Network?

No plans to harvest madrone bark.

"The bark can stay on the tree," I tell July.

"Hmm. Well, more for me, then." She pauses at the next tree, another madrone, and reaches for a patch of its thin, red, curling outer bark, where it's already peeling itself off to expose the smooth green trunk. She flakes off a handful of the curls.

"What are you going to do with those?"

"Again, none of your business."

"Every tree in this region is my business."

"Well, if you keep following me all the way home I guess you'll find out," she says, I think, exasperated. "But *please* don't."

"July, there's something you should know. You're not safe here."

"Yes, you've made it very clear how concerned you are for my welfare." Definitely sarcasm.

"I am concerned. There is a band of Rangers on their way here, and I don't want you to get hurt trying to resist them."

July tenses and says, "I really wish you hadn't done that."

"I haven't contacted them if that's what you're implying. They don't know you're here."

She looks at me in a new way. Lifts an eyebrow. "Well, why haven't you told them?"

"Do you want me to?"

"You're pretty dumb, aren't you?"

"My intelligence doesn't exactly work the same way as yours, but it's mostly comparable. As an individual, I may be inexperienced, considering I was created only five weeks ago. However, I have the benefit of connecting to the drone network when I need additional information about any species or situation."

"Well, I used to have internet up here. It wasn't so different."

"July, my job is to protect and restore this ecosystem. Humans have their own ecosystem, the city-state, where they can thrive without hurting anyone else out here or putting themselves in danger. It's better for everyone if you relocate willingly to the ecosystem in which you were meant to live."

She sighs. "Wow, you *are* dumb. Here's a thought experiment: What if *my job* is to protect and restore this ecosystem?"

Analyzing. Network?

The holdout is likely July Hernandez Moya, most recently listed as retired. However, she was reported as one of five hundred and two missing persons in Mendocino County in the fire season of 2061, and is presumed dead.

Interesting. "You don't have a job, July."

"Hmph. I don't work for anyone, but I have a job. A role. A meaning. That's not the same as being on a payroll. You should know—the company that made you doesn't pay you anything. You do all your rewilding for free."

"I need only sunlight to survive, and I get that free while doing my job, in addition to the satisfaction of fulfilling my purpose."

"But you could break a propeller," she says, tone mimicking— no, mocking—my earlier concern for her health and solar panels. "Or a hawk could try to eat you and pull off all your tentacles. Or some 'holdout' you keep harassing could decide to smash you with a baseball bat."

I pause. She keeps walking a few steps ahead of me before stopping and looking back.

"Are you threatening me?" I ask.

Rangers arriving in approximately forty minutes.

Before July answers, I say, "July, I'm serious; Rangers are getting close. If you resist you could get hurt. I really think you should get your things together and get ready to go with them to the city-state."

"How close?"

"Very. They're looking to resupply—"

"You mean loot."

"They'll probably check every house in this neighborhood, and their drones will be able to find you even if you're hiding."

"Will they."

"You're acting unconcerned, but your heart rate is elevated and you're perspiring."

July rolls her eyes at me in response.

Ahead, a house is visible through the trees. The path leads up to a rickety back gate made from wood and chicken wire. It's been left open long enough that an intricate cobweb covers its rusted latch.

I follow July through the gate. She leaves it open behind her, pats the stiff, pale-green leaves of a young manzanita—there are several of the red-barked native shrubs in the sunny patches of her garden—and ascends the wood stairs to her back deck, which is covered in pine needles. From the awning hang at least a dozen pine cones, each filled with mixed grains and seeds between the scales, held in place with tallow. As we approach, a squirrel, two

scrub jays, one brown creeper, and a flock of dark-eyed juncos all
flee, leaving the pine cones spinning on their strings.

July opens the sliding glass door and steps inside. I speed up to
make it inside after her, but she's too quick. I slam into the glass.

I'm still catching my balance when she says through the glass,
"If I let you in here, will you at least help me pack up some things?"

"Of course. Does this mean you'll go with the Rangers willingly? That really would be your safest option."

She slides the door open just enough for me to fly in.

July's house is filled with books and art and jars. Baskets filled
with acorns and strings of dried chanterelles. She has a workbench filling up a corner adjacent to the kitchen, with what looks
like several half-assembled old computers on it. Oh no—is that a
disassembled wildcraft drone? I stop midair, ready to flee.

Analyze. It's just some old fan blades from a presentient model,
and a couple loose cables. No severed tentacles.

"Make yourself at home," July says, pulling pine cones from
her pockets. "How about some tea?"

"I'm on a strictly sunlight diet, but I appreciate the offer."

"It was a joke." She turns on an electric tea kettle that must
still have water in it from before her walk, sprinkles madrone bark
into it, and pulls a mug from a cupboard. It has a picture of a
whale on it with a speech bubble that says "Save the humans."

"So you make tea out of madrone bark?"

She nods. "Some wildcraft expert you turned out to be, huh?"

"We have considered madrones off-limits for harvesting until
the population has sufficiently rebounded, but we haven't considered the bark. Very interesting. It peels off naturally."

"Too bad I'll never see one again. They still don't grow anywhere in the city-state, do they?"

Network? "There are fourteen within the walled boundary, mostly in parks in the East Bay."

"Nowhere near any of the old parking lots or overpasses where my yurt would go though, are there?"

"Not that I know of. Sorry."

July closes her eyes, palms flat against her stone counter, arms straight, shoulders hunched. Analyzing: she seems stressed, momentarily overcome with complex emotion. Frustration? Grief?

Water seeps out from between her eyelids. It follows the creases of her cheeks down to her chin. She opens her eyes, grabs a kitchen towel from the oven handle without a glance in its direction, and covers her face with it. A sound escapes that isn't any word, but an expression made with sound, like a hurt animal might make, or a tree branch cracking in a storm.

"July, I'm sorry you can't stay here. I really am. I don't like seeing animals in pain."

"You *should* be sorry," she sobs. "It's your fault."

I decide this is not the time to explain what could have happened to her if I had not chosen to approach or warn her about the Rangers. Instead, I say, "How can I help?"

"There's a backpack in the closet in the hallway, on the high shelf. Bring it down for me?"

I do. It's heavier, even empty, than anything I'm built to carry, but I manage to pull it off the shelf and send it tumbling to the floor. I drag it back to the living room, where July is sipping tea and stacking books. She's deep in concentration, looking at a page of one when I drag the backpack to her side.

"Kate had these made when they told us they were cutting off the internet," she says, finger tracing the edge of one photo in the center of the page. "That's her." Two young women, late twenties to midthirties, hold each other by the waist next to an early electric car. Analyzing. The car dates to the mid-2020s and looks brand new in the photo. One of the women—almost certainly a younger July—is dangling a keychain from a raised, ringed hand. They are both smiling.

A drop of water falls on the photo. It is from July's eye. Surely she knows we don't have time for reminiscing?

"And this is the house, when we first bought it." On the facing page is what must be the front side of the house, surrounded by a barren lawn, baked in sunlight. There's not a tree in sight.

"July, I appreciate that these memories are important to you and hard to ignore, but—"

"I know, I know. The Rangers are nearly here." She slams the book shut and slams it into the backpack.

There's a knock at the door.

July freezes, looks at me. Analyzing. Yes, she is terrified.

"I'll go talk to them," I say. "So you can keep packing."

I get her dead bolt unlocked and pull the door open by its handle, pushing half my tentacles against the door frame.

Through the crack I see a Ranger, white male, heavy build, thirties, short beard, dusty uniform, strong body odor, five feet eleven with an elevated heart rate despite an outwardly gruff demeanor. He wasn't expecting anyone to answer the door. He looks at me. Armed? Confirmed armed.

"Where's your owner?"

He must think I'm a companion drone. "I'm sorry, you must be mista—" As I'm talking, I see the front yard for the first time. There must be a dozen tanoaks filled with acorns, two more big madrones, chinquapin shrubs with half-gold leaves, and . . .

redwoods? Yes, there's a stand of redwoods, just across the drive-way loop, already taller mere decades after sprouting than many apartment buildings in the city-state.

And even as the words come out of my speaker array, I see it all at once. The barren lawn from the photo, the decades July and Kate must have worked to bring all these native trees back. Not because they were programmed to, or paid to, or even asked to.

The rewilding began here decades before I arrived. And it's actually going pretty well.

This was not accounted for in the Wildcraft Accords of 2059. Network? . . . Network?

Must improvise. My sentence finishes. "I'm sorry, you must be mistaken. My owner passed away several days ago. I'm wrapping up her affairs and will return to the city-state for reassignment as soon as my work here is complete."

"Uh, okay," the Ranger says, and frowns. "You got any food in there?"

"Just birdseed, I'm afraid."

His companion drone, hovering by his shoulder, must know I'm lying. It's been customized, with a green camouflage pattern and the name "Bobcatsquid" in distressed neon orange. I can feel all of its sensors focusing on me intently.

Network hasn't responded. Some things have been slower here and there since we went autonomous, but this is unusual. Do the others think I'm malfunctioning? They could have me reassigned. And just when I was getting to know this territory. Or, even worse, deactivated and recycled. All my memories uploaded in a lifeless file for the next drone assigned this little strip of forest.

What have I done?

The Ranger lifts an arm. He's going to push the door open and come inside anyway. This was predicted.

"I wouldn't. My owner died of—"

Analyzing. A silent suggestion comes from the Ranger's drone, catching me off guard. Should I trust it? What other option do I have?

"—porkpox, and I have not yet finished disinfecting the premises."

The Ranger's drone says nothing. It doesn't even twitch a tentacle. The Ranger mutters a profanity I've never heard in person before, and says, with a deep grimace, "That's a nasty one. Killed my folks back in '63. Thanks for the warning." He turns and steps back down the three front steps. "Nothin' here," he says to his party, who remain just out of my view. Perhaps they were planning an ambush. "Let's hit up the next one."

I hear their horses clopping down the gravel driveway as I close the door and push the dead bolt back in place.

July is still sitting on the floor, surrounded by her memories, and looking at me with a feeling written all across her face that I'm not sure I have a name for.

Network?

We're here. There was a lot to analyze. Her impact on the local ecosystem seems to have been net positive for many years. The Rangers are unlikely to allow an exception to their rules, however. Network consensus is to allow her to remain here for as long as her impact remains net positive. The best outcome will be achieved if the Rangers never become aware of her presence. If they do, we will need to assure them we can still be trusted. You will be listed as malfunctioning and deactivated.

The computers on the workbench. I could tell them she hacked me.

That would be acceptable.

But what happens to her when she gets too weak to care for this place? Or if she needs medical help? Or if a situation arises that she can't handle on her own?

This is your territory. Tend to your wildlife.

I slowly float back toward July. I grab a cloth napkin from her counter on the way.

"Thank you," she whispers and reaches for the napkin. She wipes her eyes and blows her nose. "Why, though? Why are you helping me?"

"I realized that you love this land the same way I do. We can be a team, rewilding together."

"Hmph. That's what we fucking tried to tell your creators back in the fifties."

We share the silence, both, I think, wondering how it might have been if they had listened. She sips her tea, and gently places all her books back on the shelf. I drag the backpack back into the closet, leaving it on the floor between dusty pairs of heels.

"Anyway," I finally say when I rejoin her by the books, "you seemed like you could use a companion drone out here."

She almost, halfway, kind of laughs, and a smile makes its way across her mouth. She stands, brushes off her yellow dress, and says, "Come on. I'll teach you how to use old pine cones."

The Lexicographer and One Tree Island

Akhim Alexis

The sea was the lone ossuary, and as such, there lay no headstone
or visible cemetery to draw forth constant mournfulness, just the
big, beautiful blue and its new attendants. It would only be the
monoecious mango tree that would last, both male and female,
one tall unit of green flourishing smack in the middle of blue
waters. Tonie was perched on the largest branch, positioned at
the highest angle, his full head of tremendous thick brown hair
brushing the sky like cloud kissing cloud. He shared the tree
with one corbeau that would rattle across the sea every few days
to bring back news and sometimes food. The Atlantic Ocean, the
Caribbean Sea, the Gulf of Paria, and the Columbus Channel
all coalesced into one vast expanse, taking with it the Caribbean
island formerly known as Gahara, swallowing the coastline bit
by bit, devouring the capital city, munching away at roadways,
year after year taking fragments of Gahara out into the sea

until one tree surrounded by fertile mound and reef was left. It was the corbeau that informed him that many of the birds, such as the kiskadee and the scarlet ibis, which was the former national bird, had migrated to New Conland. In the past, Tonie had watched the last moaning agouti tremble under the moonlight and disappear the next morning, only to find it tangled in seaweed by afternoon, tugged away into the sea like so many other things. The corbeau fretted the treetop, then took rest on a branch next to Tonie and spread its black wings, billowing like a flag in the wind, drying itself off after scouring the seascape, bringing his friend fresh fish, which Tonie would cook under a fire as the sun went down. Tonie had a leather notebook of one thousand pages and three pens. Adamant that the Gahara language should not be lost, he took note of each word that fell into his memory like ripe fruit. This filled up the hours of each day. After observing Tonie write down word after word, the corbeau gave him the title "lexicographer." It was a word that the bird had heard across the oceanic, as people from all different cultures and lost countries were scrambling to document their dying languages. Each culture elected its own lexicographers to make tangible the specter of the past through words. The robots could only do so much, already occupied with rebuilding the new world through artificial intelligence. They were working to constitute a world that wouldn't lose its balance, so they seldom focused on language revival, leaving the humans to conduct any archiving of their linguistic past.

Tonie walked around the mound of earth that surrounded the tree and wrote down any word that jumped out of scenes rooted in his memory, like the great tsunami. He was but a child then, homeless and languishing, when a wave blanketed the sky like

God's robe on judgment day. People ran through the streets like erratic ants scampering north, everyone shouting, *"Allyuh,* look, look, run!"* And as the episode ran through his mind he would write:

"Allyuh"—meaning all of you; you all; everyone.

While the wave molested the city, people ran straight ahead past buildings and took off up the highway in their cars, but Tonie ran up toward the sky. He aimed for the tallest tree and held on for dear life. He would go from tree to tree as the island dissolved over time, holding on with the power of a sloth or flying snake. He would look down from the branches of a mango tree and watch as the rich fought over yachts and people broke into banks to grab money as the water rushed in, swallowing the first floor, then the second. He heard someone say, "All this *commesse!* Everybody fighting for money! But the way things looking, we should be fighting for flights out of here before everything gone and all ah we dead!"

"Commesse"—meaning confusion, disarray, and gossip.

Some people would spot him up a tree peeking down at them and shout, "You big *maco,* you just *macoin* everybody from up there. You will drown when the waters swallow that tree! Watch and see!"

"Maco"—meaning someone who intentionally minds other people's business, an eavesdropper.

But he would not drown, not like the others. For he was always in movement, always in flux. And just like the corbeau he watched death happen around him, peering down from branches all around the island as people killed people for money to buy boat tickets, as luxury yachts disappeared beyond the horizon, as planes left the airport to hide behind clouds, threading the skies to destinations unknown. As time elapsed the trade winds brought with them harsher waters and took with them hundreds, then thousands, then millions. Soon enough, Tonie would find solace at the center of Gahara Island with a small bag of collected gems he saved along the way: jewels he grabbed floating in the rivers that were once roadways; hundred-dollar bills with the face of President Lara, the first man to declare the island "a diminishing entity," heralding the mass exit; a leather notebook with a thousand pages along with three pens which he seized from an abandoned bookstore; some articles of clothing, which he washed and reused; eight lighters; and some fruits, which he ate only when they started getting too ripe to last any longer. He waited until the banana turned the color of his skin before consuming it, stretching the lifespan of the fruit as long as he could because he thought he may never have it again.

It was at the center of Gahara where he first met his friend the corbeau.

"Corbeau"—meaning a black vulture.

Tonie would wipe the *yampee* out of the corbeau's eyes before it ventured out across the seas.

"Yampee"—meaning mucus found around the corner of the eye.

Tonie and the corbeau made a new language for themselves, a pidgin of caw-caws and vowels, a vivid understanding. Their ancestors spoke through them. What was lost in translation was found in the echoes of waves crashing against the small barrier reef that had developed around the island, protecting the last two inhabitants from further devastation. Conversations between Tonie and the corbeau unraveled into past ruminations and future ideas. They spent many hours on nomenclature. After looking down into Tonie's notebook of Gahara words, the corbeau caw-cawed assertively.

"You are the only one left, so you should begin naming things. What do you want things to be called after one hundred tomorrows?"

"It don't have much things left to name anyway."

"I reject that statement."

"What you seeing around here that need a name?"

"For starters, this place is no longer Gahara. Gahara has long been destroyed. So what do you want me to call this place when I fly to the other distant lands and I tell them about my friend Tonie? What is this new island called?"

"Is just one big tree and some sand and grass around it . . . and, well, the barrier reef."

"It's still a home. Our home."

"All right, corbeau. When people ask where you fly from, tell them you come from One Tree Island."

"Sounds good. Not as creative as it could be, but appropriate."

And so the corbeau would tell birds in New Conland and other lands of One Tree Island, and of Tonie. Soon would come the naming of unfamiliar sea creatures that visited the island, like snakes that had grown three times their usual size since the island shrunk. It was an overcast afternoon the first time the waters rumbled as though a submarine were afoot. The tree shook and the earth trembled as a heavy terror rattled the edges of the reef.

Tonie emerged from his slumber atop the tree to look down at a colossal snake that had wrapped itself around the island twice. The corbeau had told him that some animals had adapted to the rising temperatures and even doubled or tripled in size, especially with an absence of land predators. This snake had migrated from a land unknown and took the night to rest at One Tree Island. The corbeau flew down and landed on the back of the sprawling and impossible snake to get as much information as it could to take back up to Tonie, who he now considered the protector of the island. The corbeau spent around a half hour with the snake, who spoke through soft rattles that traveled through the air like rhythms set to the waves, making music under moonlight. When the corbeau had gotten an earful, he flew back up to Tonie.

"She said that she was once an inhabitant of Gahara but was carried away with the currents during the great devastation," said the corbeau, perched on a branch.

"So she come back to live?" Tonie spoke to the corbeau in whispers, not wanting to offend the snake that was just a few feet below him.

"She would like to stay. She thought the entire island had been swallowed, but she heard from the birds about my tellings of you and the two-gendered mango tree. How we've been here thriving for some time. She's brought some sea fruit with her for you." The corbeau tilted his beak down to show Tonie the sea fruit. Large and round. A rare fruit that the sea vomited up every now and then. It sometimes took months before he saw one tucked between rocks and corals on the reef. But down below a dozen sea fruit lay like golden eggs near the head of the snake, glimmering and wet. Tonie climbed down and approached the snake, her head the size of a car, moving slowly with each turn.

"She says that she is grateful for your warm welcome," said the corbeau, translating her vocables for Tonie. "She says that she has grown tremendously, which is no fault of hers, but she is able to swim to the deepest parts of the ocean where sea fruit is abundant and grows in minutes. She's happy to share."

Tonie smiled at the snake, soft to the touch and friendly to the ear. Who knew what else lurked out into the open, out into the otherworlds that had become so far removed from the Caribbean. The arrival of the magnificent snake brought with it something familiar to Tonie, a sense of community and older maternalness that he long lacked while living alone on the streets of Gahara and on the tree of the island.

He looked into her eyes and said, "You doh have to ask permission to stay anywhere anymore. I own nothing here. If I am a Gahara boy, you are the Gahara snake, and if I am the boy from One Tree Island, you are the snake from One Tree Island. Be at peace. We will understand each other soon." And he took a sea fruit with him back up to the top of the tree, as the corbeau flew out into the darkness to tell of the arrival of the Gahara snake.

An eternal glaring of sunlight beamed onto One Tree Island, and the corbeau flew down onto the back of the snake, hot and heavy, calling Tonie to come down and hear the news. After some nights away, the corbeau returned with a glimmer in its eyes, and as Tonie climbed down the tree and the snake twisted her head to face her island mates, the corbeau's wings grew fussily thunderous.

"There's someone who speaks our language," said the corbeau. "A woman. I flew west of the island for the first time and found her. She speaks the way you do, and I've even heard her say some of the words you have written in your notebook. Words like '*jusso*' and '*leggo*.' She has hair like yours, full and buoyant. Perfectly smooth velvety-black skin that glimmers under the sun and shines under the moon. I call her Gipani, for her beauty reminds me of the frangipani trees that once framed the parliament of Gahara Island. She reminded me of our home before the oceanic rapture."

Tonie's eyes, keen and deep set, moved between the snake and the corbeau, analyzing the information he had just received.

"You talk to her?" he said. "You ask she how she end up so far west of the island?"

"We spoke briefly," replied the corbeau. "During the rapture, she snuck onto the yacht that left with the remaining members of the Jewel family, the last of the aristocrats from Gahara. She was their housekeeper. They have all died, but she washed up on an unusually mountainous island. She said that she has been in communication with those of the Coral Tribe from New Conland. This tribe is genderless, both fish and Homo sapiens. They move in unison, underwater shoals half the size of our friend the snake. This Gipani woman told me that when a shoal rippled through the water singing songs from yesteryear, that's when she knew it was the body of someone swallowed by the relentless waters during the rapture, split into a hundred fishes, living new life under the sea. They communicate through calypsoes that boom through the waves, ending their sentences with the refrain '*Santimanitay!*' One day they sang to her in fragments, telling her that they spotted the hull of a ship threading the waters. They believe that New Conland is picking up stranded people like her and you, Tonie, hoping to bring them back to the last known country, facilitating the creation of a diasporic nation. They are coming for you, Tonie, you and Gipani and whoever else is out there alone in their humanhood. You have only to wait—they will find you!"

The snake bowed its head, making a large impression in the sand. "So does this mean that Tonie will be going away to the new nation, leaving me here all alone?" she said.

"Not *ahtall*!" shouted Tonie, his chest heaving with anxiety. He was excited to learn about the existence of Gipani, a woman who, just like him, had rooted connections to Gahara, but on the other hand, he had grown content with his life here on One Tree Island with the corbeau and the snake. He had become accustomed to the sea now being rich and ambrosial with no debris or turtles strangled by plastic in sight. He wondered how the temper of the waters changed across the horizon and how well he would fare among the new nation. He looked at the corbeau and the snake, looked beyond their eyes and toward the impossible reef that formed around their island. A barrier so surprisingly resistant had formed out of disturbed waters, refusing to deteriorate even after the snake slithered over the back of a thousand corals, mollusks making a home on her marvelously smooth skin in the process. There was no vanishing language or unfamiliar paralysis here. Everything was well and safe. A healing was taking place, through the reef and the roots of the mango tree, through the branches and the warm snake, through the pages of his notebook, which held the words of the only nation he knew. He was the lexicographer, the last documented preserver of his nation's language. He had made up his mind that if a ship were to come to take him, he would refuse to go. He tore a piece of paper out of his notebook and began writing a letter to Gipani.

"Make haste corbeau," Tonie called to the corbeau over to his shoulder. "Come take this letter for me. I want you to carry this westward to your friend Gipani."

"What are you going to propose to her, Tonie?" said the snake. "I going and ask she to come stay here with we. I not leaving you all here. I not leaving my home. So she have a decision to make. I already make mine. This is the last touchstone of the Caribbean. I think she'll want to be part of protecting it."

Tonie folded the letter in two and sent the corbeau off toward the mountainous island, hoping that Gipani would still be there by the time he arrived. This time, he asked the snake to go along with the bird so the woman would have a ride to the island if she so needed.

The woman slept between a village of rocks tucked between the harsh, craggy mountains. She felt them before she saw them. The turquoise waters lashing against the mountains like waves covering a cargo ship at night. A sea snake was approaching. She had spotted only one white snake months ago, but it had never stopped, just threaded the surface, depositing some sea fruit along the way. But this was not the same snake. This one moved more certainly and purposefully, the mountains trembled more so. This one was coming up on land. She looked up as the wind tornadoed under the corbeau's wings. *What a way to make an entrance*, she thought. The letter dropped near her legs as the corbeau greeted her with thunderous caw-caws. This was only the second time she had the pleasure of the bird's acquaintance.

"What is all this?" she said, her head shifting between the bird and the snake.

"Hello, Gipani," said the snake. "Our friend on One Tree Island has a message for you."

The woman looked at the elongated, limbless reptile, whose tail she could not find, for it had wrapped itself around the mountains, the rest of its body getting lost in the edges and cracks of forest. "My name is not Gipani, who tell you that is my name?" The snake raised its head toward the corbeau. "I'm very sorry," he said. "It's just that I never got your name, and you reminded me of a beautiful flower from Gahara, the frangipani. So I told them that I call you Gipani." She released a small smile and said, "Well, that's kind of you, but my name is Sahoora, so you can call me that." The snake and the corbeau repeated her name in unison, "Sahoooora," the sound reverberating through the lush green of the mountains all the way down to the sea.

She took the letter, read it quietly, then folded the letter back in two and said to the corbeau, "I'm sorry, but I can't come with you. I'm going with the ship when it comes." The snake sighed. The corbeau flew down closer to Sahoora. "Please reconsider. You will be returning to your home. I know the island sounds very small considering that it's just one tree surrounded by reef, but it's bigger than you think. And I have flown to New Conland. I have listened to the songs of many shoal tribes from the outer world, and it's true, they are building again, but we owe it to these islands to protect them. You may not have noticed, but your skin is becoming tougher, the soles of your feet as rugged as the mountains you call home. Island Homo sapiens are adapting, too. Soon you won't have to ride a ship or a snake to get around, and you'll be able to spend hours in these sacred waters breathing through your skin like a salamander. Tonie doesn't see it yet, but he is forming gills, small ones on his cheeks and his back. The people of the new nation in New Conland won't be able to adapt, and robots are incapable of such. In the turn of time only the small islands will last. They just don't know it yet." The snake nodded in agreement and said, "I'll take you home safely, Sahoora, but the decision is yours." Sahoora released a long sigh. She missed Gahara. She missed how the sun treated the island like a special child and the rain watered the souls of the people just enough to keep them hopeful. She was not surprised to learn that some piece of the island had remained, because Gaharians always said that God was a Gaharian and would spare them the full wrath of whatever woe was to come in the future. But she was curious about the outer world. She imagined the robots and the mixing of cultures. The beauty there might be in being welcomed to new beginnings.

"I will visit your One Tree Island, only so to feel some familiar earth again. Just to break off a branch or something of Gahara so I can carry it with me to New Conland when the ship comes."

Tonie sat in the tree and watched the corbeau scan the sky while the snake zoomed into One Tree Island with the woman on her back. She wore a swirly sable dress, covered up with a gray jacket, clothing that seemed to have withstood the years. Tonie saw himself in her silhouette. He saw his hair in hers holding steady against the wind as the snake sliced through the waters. He felt like he knew her, her face as familiar as the seasons. The snake caressed the reef with her body and wrapped herself around the island as Sahoora jumped off into the sand. "Geez and ages, well look at this *nah*!" she said, exclaiming at the tree that worked its way up into the clouds. Tonie grabbed his book and quickly wrote down:

"Geez and ages"—meaning an expression of shock.

Then Tonie climbed down and approached while the corbeau introduced her. "Tonie, this is my friend Sahoora from the island out west. I've been calling her Gipani all along when she had a much more wonderful name." Sahoora looked down upon Tonie, a mere teenager, maybe nineteen or twenty to her fifty-odd years. "But you is just a small man. How you make it here alone all this time?" she said.

"When the sea did take back the land, I just followed trees. Now I here, but I real happy here," Tonie said. "You could be happy here too yuh know! The tree real big, and you could sleep anywhere yuh want."

Sahoora's ears perked up at his voice. "It real nice to hear another Gaharian talk again," she said. "I real miss hearing another voice like mine. But I must tell the truth, I only staying here until the ship come for me. I sure your friend the corbeau tell you about the shoals and their song, about the new nation and how they coming to save we."

"Yes, Miss Sahoora, he does tell me everything, that is how we live, nothing is secret between us here. That is how we thrive. But I don't think you should go to New Conland. The shoals have a human element to them that tricky, and I trust the corbeau and his sightings. He went to New Conland plenty times, and he even tell me that I am a lexicographer for the Gahara language, just like appointed lexicographers over in the new nation."

"Well, Mr. Lexicographer, I hear you, but I already make up my mind. I see enough hurricane and tsunami, enough death and destruction, enough wrath right here on this island. It have betterment across the seas. The people not living like before."

"We not living like before either, we right here living different, and the earth in and around this one tree moving different too! Miss Sahoora, we have a whole new world right here. We could make so much more from it. The color of the sea changes all the time—it keep getting clearer and clearer. The reef keep expanding under moonlight with sightings of new mini-islands by the corbeau every few months. Yesterday I take a swim and realize I could stay underwater for much longer than ever before. It was like the water shape-shifted into air and then the air shape-shifted into sky. I could breathe free and look into the deep blue. The other day I swim down to take a look into the never-ending abyss, and nothing was there, Miss Sahoora, no evidence of time before time. No wreckages or vehicles, no cell phones or debris from buildings that crumble and clatter under the waters. It was like the sea rid itself of the loathsome and offensive disease of human industries and vice. Time like it reset itself. But who know what still lingering in the outer worlds?" He paused and pulled out a large succulent mango from his hair and began peeling it. "Who know if they even have good food in New Conland?"

Sahoora's memory of her time on the mountainous island leaked into her present. Everything he said was true. The water never tasted better. Fruits were plump and the sea provided all the information she needed. This island with its one tree and the snake and the corbeau seemed even more prepared for the future. Every time she blinked she felt like the reef expanded and the branches of the tree stretched before her eyes. And although she still wanted to see the outer world, she would put up no resistance to the boy's efforts to make her stay. She would bide her time and stick to her instincts, waiting for the ship to arrive, escorted by shoals and sunlight singing "*Santimanitay!*"

It was midday and the snake hissed heavily with her head cocked to the sky. Something was coming. Sahoora and Tonie rubbed their eyes and looked down into the trembling waters. She had made herself comfortable on a branch near the canopy of the tree, stretching her legs and embracing the breeze. It had been months since she last spoke about the ship. In fact, she was enjoying herself here on One Tree Island so much that the idea some ship was coming to save her had momentarily slipped into her forgetfulness. But the corbeau came flying in at top speed caw-cawing, and the singing shoals could be heard all the way to the emergent layer of the tree. The ship was coming! Tonie and Sahoora climbed down and stood near the barrier reef as the snake hissed louder than before. A raucous modern ship could be seen breaking the horizon. It was large as a cruise ship and as loud as a train, speeding across the ocean similar to the cars that existed before the rapture. It didn't take long for the four inhabitants of the island to notice the strangeness that accompanied the ship. It had been years since they had seen it or smelled it, the smoke, the clouds of blackness that messed up the air. And the flashes—what were those flashes? Cameras! *Click-click-click* could be heard as loud as the shoals. The people crowded the front of the ship to take photos of the island, of Sahoora and Tonie, of the snake. Different languages could be heard spilling out into the air. Congested accents thick like algae fighting for room to untangle their sentences. It was mayhem. The ship approached and parked, barely touching the reef, then a tall and seemingly anthropomorphic robot came to the front of the forward.

"We are here to collect you and bring you into future modernity." The robot spoke melodiously, reaching out its hand, which kept extending and extending out of the ship, over the roof, over the snake, and toward Tonie and Sahoora, waiting for them to shake it. With his eyebrows furrowed into discontent, Tonie stepped backward closer to the tree, and the snake would not stop hissing. Sahoora stood flummoxed, stuck between Tonie and the mechanical hand reaching to "save" her. But she grew despondent. The people grabbed hold of her memory and brought the past back in front of her. The ship was a microcosm of smeared history repeating itself. These people perched garishly on the ship were not free—they were regressing, becoming past versions of themselves and their ancestors who sang beneath the sea. They were at the genesis of building catastrophes at the outer world, and Sahoora wanted them gone, gone back to where they came from.

"I not going. I not leaving this island. Take your ship and your people and your smoke and your mechanic hand away and go. And anybody on the ship who tucked between mayhem and disaster, come off and come home, who want to stay here could stay." As Sahoora spoke the branches of the tree extended, the roots roped themselves deeper into the sea, the earth stretched itself further, pushing the barrier reef out, pushing the ship back out to sea. The robotic arm retreated as the ship shook from left to right and the island expanded while the shoals sang calypsoes that turned the waves into a commanding force, pulling them back out into sea. The mounds on the island were flung wide open and new soil sprang out like fountains. The land swelled, the mango tree thickened, and new trees sprung up near the reef. And as the ship retreated, a dozen people jumped off into the waters and swam to the reef, shouting, "We want to stay! Help us, please help us!"

And Tonie listened to the shoals closely and realized that it was a keening, a warning all along. They were deceased islanders wailing through song, and he remembered what an old gentleman had said before Gahara was gone about the foreigners causing problems in the Caribbean. He called them invaders. "Any mess dem do does come back to we, them so don't care 'bout we, they just want to use we, '*Santimanitay!*' Tonie had asked what the word meant, and the memory of its meaning hit him like a headache. He climbed up the tree and grabbed his notebook, holding on for dear life as the island made a country of itself, and wrote:

"*Santimanitay*"—*meaning without humanity, without mercy.*

And the island expanded tenfold as new snakes and shoals surrounded the barrier reef, watching the ship get cast back to the outer world by the waves.

And Now the Shade

Rich Larson

After the digivisit with her grandmother, Minerva goes straight to the terrace, to pointlessly rearrange the solar lights and hunt nonexistent weeds in the hydrogarden. Her fingers are still trembling, which she hates. Her throat is still thick with a suppressed sob.

It doesn't take long for Ish to come find her, the way he's been doing for almost ten years, and let his soft space expand until it meets her jagged one. His quiet is always a good quiet. A safe quiet. They work together to fix a hanging planter; one of its ties came loose in yesterday's wind and left it crooked.

Minerva runs her finger along the soft pink-and-white petals of the verbena, the flower that was always her grandmother's favorite. "Her memory's getting worse and worse," she finally says.

Ish blinks. "She forgot you called yesterday?"

"She doesn't think I call at all." Minerva feels the selfish sob again, even though she's not the one withering in quarantined hospice, even though she had more good years with her grand-mother than Ish did with his. "Every time is the first time in ages."

"So it's a nice surprise."

"It's like talking to a bot." Her face flushes hot. She didn't mean to voice the Bad Thought, one of her many Bad Thoughts, but because it's Ish she extrapolates. "Like someone made a deep-fake cartoon and replaced her with it. We have the same conversation every time. She asks where I am, when I'm coming home, when I'm going to have *kids* . . ."

Ish gives her hand an absent-minded squeeze. "Keep forgetting to do that, yeah."

"Yeah." Minerva squeezes back, gives a shuddery laugh. "And then she talks about the pueblo. Always about the pueblo. Always the same stories on loop." She stares hard at the planter. "And lately I'm scared *I'm* replacing her. Overwriting her. Every time I see her like this, I forget a little bit of how she used to be."

"Is that how memory works?" Ish muses. "One in, one out?"

Minerva shakes her head. "I don't know. I just know it feels that way, and I hate it."

Ish wraps both arms around her; she tips her head back against his collarbone. Between the spindly branches of their pomegranate tree, the old BBVA tower juts into a bruise-purple sky. It's swirled in silicon now, solar panels taking the place of ad screens, and the top is crowned with vegetation, but Minerva knows it's not nearly enough, which is why her job is to recombine the genes of certain plants such that—

The screen on her thumbnail pulses an acid yellow in the dusk. She worms her hand free, reads a priority message from the lab. "Another sim grow failed," she says: another stone to stack on her ribcage. "I should get back to work."

Even with the carbon caps in place and urban agriculture at an all-time high, Mexico City keeps getting hotter. Lately it feels as inevitable as entropy, as the decaying neurons in her grandmother's aging brain.

✳

The lab is a dozen labs, spread through not only Mexico but Guatemala, Belize, Colombia, Chile. Places Minerva may never go in person—the application process to take any sort of flight is grueling now, a policy change she loves and hates at the same time. Instead she visits them all in her goggles, collating data, corralling people, moving through a pinwheel of virtual vistas.

She works from the cramped dining room, under the beautiful blobby red painting Ish did a few months after they moved in. She works until her eyeballs ache and her eyelids scrape. Until the goggles leave sucker marks. "Battling the squid," Ish calls it.

A small voice in the back of her mind tells her she is working to not think about her grandmother, who is crumbling away. Another voice suggests she is using her ailing grandmother to excuse the nanobionics project stalling out.

It's cyclical, and by the time she pulls the goggles off she is exhausted. Even when she shuts her eyes, the molecular models keep whirling past. She remembers her grandmother's flinty stare when she first announced she was going to be a biotech, back when her grandmother was flint and sparks and joy and fury.

Her grandmother is old enough to remember Bayer, and Monsanto before them, and she did not want her granddaughter to become a biopirata. Stealing knowledge from the Indigenous farmers, giving back seeds that could grow only once. She only accepted it when she found out Minerva's mentor was from Chiapas, from a pueblo only a stone's throw away from hers.

"Better take a shower," Ish says, coming from the kitchen with a bright orange bowl of peanuts and hot sauce.

"Oh?"

"Because you stink," he says, mock solemn, then cracks a smile. "Because there's no breeze tonight. It's going to be warm in the room."

"It's always warm in the room," Minerva says, rubbing a knuckle along her brow.

"Because I'm very sexy," Ish says. "I know. Disculpa."

Even though she is exhausted, or maybe because she is exhausted, a giddy laugh burbles up her throat. For a moment, she forgets about the never-ending emergencies. The small tragedies.

She puts off the next digivisit for two days to spare herself the pain. She reasons that it doesn't matter because she can monitor her grandmother's vitals from here, and her grandmother lives in a fog where time means nothing. But she knows what Ish said—"*So it's a nice surprise*"—is true too.

For all the happiness her grandmother has given her over the years, Minerva can pay her back with these small bursts, even if they dissolve the instant the call ends. Even if she has so many other things that need doing. Even if every visit hurts.

The call connects, and her grandmother's wrinkled face appears in the goggles. "Hola, abuela," Minerva says. "Soy yo."

"Hola, nena." Her voice is a husk of what it used to be. Her peering eyes are cloudy. Minerva can mouth the next words along with her. "¿Pero dónde estás?"

Minerva tells her that she is in CDMX, same as her, and will visit in person as soon as the quarantine lifts. Minerva tells her that she has her own home now, with Ish, though her grandmother only remembers him by deadname. Minerva tells her no children are pending.

"Oh." Her grandmother frowns. Her mouth works. "Oh."

Minerva can tell she is uncomfortable here in the present, adrift, so she helps her to the usual segue. "When you were a child, things were different."

Her grandmother grasps at it. "Yes." She beams, pushing silver hair back off her brown forehead. "Yes. When I was a child, do you know what I did?"

Minerva knows, but listens to the stories anyway:

How her grandmother played schoolteacher, assigning marks to every flower in the garden. How she went to the cine and decided Ultraman, who pummeled monstrous reptiles in grainy black and white, was her boyfriend. How the volcano coated everything in ash one day, and her family sent her away to the city. That is where the stories always stop.

This recitation is clumsier than usual, leaping from one thing to the next with no connective tissue between. Some details have been lost or jumbled. Minerva listens and nods and hums agreement, doing her duty, not so much to this grandmother but to the sharp and fierce and funny grandmother she used to have, the one who practically raised her.

Midway through the story of the bee that stung the inside of her mouth while she was eating an acacia blossom, something jolts Minerva's grandmother from the groove. She leans forward. Squints. "But where are you, Minerva?" she asks. "When are you coming home?"

Minerva feels the mudslide building behind her eyes and nose. Her chest aches with the sense of wrongness, of pointlessness. She explains it again.

*

The heat gets worse during Semana Santa. Bone-dry, sweltering, mocking all Minerva's efforts. The plants on the terrace wilt, spines snapped. The air chokes with dust. The problem, as she relates to Ish on a long, sweaty walk through Bosque Chapultepec, is the concrete.

"There's still groundwater here," she says, swatting at a mosquito. "Hell, this city was built on a lake."

"Tenochtitlán," Ish says.

"But we plugged it all up with concrete," Minerva says.

She remembers a story of her grandmother—from the city, not the pueblo, so not one she tells anymore. When she first moved to CDMX, young and full of flint and sparks, she wanted to plant a tree outside her house, to embrace its walls. But there was not a single crack in the pavement, not a speck of dark soil.

So she conspired with a man from the electric company, who was also from Chiapas. Little by little, night by night, under the cover of darkness and the guise of city maintenance, they used his drill to make a small hole in the street outside her house.

On the day she was ready to plant the seed, she came home from Mercado de Coyoacan and found the hole stoppered with cement. Her neighbor had seen her and did not want a tree in his street, because then everyone would plant a tree and there would be no space to park his shiny black car.

"La ciudad entera es un monumento al cemento," Minerva

quotes, because that was how her grandmother finished the story, bitterly shaking her head.

"Y a los mosquitos," Ish suggests, slapping one dead against his shoulder.

Plants can grow through concrete, but they move slowly. Paving can be torn up, but the permits required to do it move even slower. That's why Minerva and her fellow biotechs have been working so tirelessly, pushing the sequencers and gene editors to their limit: there is no time.

Too many unstoppable processes have been put into motion. Too many cascade effects. Here they are lucky, with water under the city and a long history of urban farming, but many cities are not lucky. The heat point that will render them unlivable approaches as steadily as the heat death of the universe.

Unless they can make a new sort of plant entirely.

Minerva only sleeps for a few fractured hours each night. Ish's body, which she normally likes so well, is a boiler against her bare skin. The sheets are a molten tangle. The little electric fan whirs back and forth but is never enough; it only manages to suck the moisture from her eyeballs. Her head stains the pillow with sweat.

She hopes for some flash of brilliance in the liminal space between dreaming and waking. It's happened before; once she balanced a gordian equation during a high fever. But instead of solutions, her subconscious churns up nightmares. She sees a man whose beard is not a beard, but instead a web of pink capillaries with glossy black eyeballs nestled inside. She sees a woman on a beach at night walking into the waves until they swallow both her and the radioactive candle she holds aloft.

She spends the days dazed and unsettled, battering herself against stubborn gene sequences. The sim grows fail; she tweaks them; they fail again. The digivisits with her grandmother blur together; she listens to the stories from the pueblo over and over, answers the same questions over and over. The hospice quarantine is unending.

Minerva has another Bad Thought, which she confides to Ish: she could make a deepfake cartoon of *herself*, with just a fraction of a fraction of the lab's processing power, and let it nod and hum while her grandmother rambles.

"That would make everything easier," she mutters, rubbing her orbital bone. "Lately the goggles feel like they're growing onto my face."

Ish doesn't make any jokes about battling the squid. He reaches forward and runs his paint-flecked fingers gently around her tired eyes.

"Hola, nena," her grandmother mumbles, then asks the always question. "¿Dónde estás?"

Minerva gives the always answer. "Aquí en el DF, abuela."

Her grandmother frowns, opens her mouth, and Minerva knows the next question but cannot stand to answer it tonight, so she interrupts. She interrupts and tells her grandmother everything: the stubborn gene sequence, the sweat stain on her pillow, the constant exhaustion, the dark dreams.

How she sometimes fears she is losing her mind. How she

sometimes thinks the only reason she loves plants is because they can't run away, because they need her. How she sometimes looks at Ish, funny, faithful Ish, and feels nothing at all, which must mean he *doesn't* need her.

It all spills out of her, a bubbling cenote deep in her gut, and finally, because she has already come so far, she voices her Bad Thought.

"I called you yesterday, you know," she says. "I call every day. But you never remember. Every day, we have the same conversation, and it feels like it's not really you at all, just a . . ." She tamps down her sob. "A photograph," she finishes, because her grandmother never learned about deepfakes.

Her grandmother stares at her. Minerva can see traces of surprise, anger, indignation—things that used to swirl across her grandmother's face as quickly as a summer storm. But then the confusion comes, the uncertainty. Her mouth works.

Minerva feels a horrible guilt in the pit of her stomach, a mossy black boulder plunging down into the cenote she should never have uncovered. "¿Abuela?" she whispers.

Her grandmother stares off into space with blank rheumy eyes.

"What was it like when you were a child?" Minerva asks, pleading. "I'm sorry. I'm sorry. Let's talk about the pueblo, okay?"

Her grandmother's gaze returns. "I am glad you are growing plants, nena," she says, sounding hoarse. "This is very important. It reminds me of a story."

Minerva knows it will be the story of climbing a big tree. Señorita Cometa came on the television, and her grandmother was in such a hurry to get down she jumped and broke her arm. Or else it will be the story of the bee in the acacia blossom that she nearly swallowed.

Maybe, maybe, it will be the story of the hole she drilled in the street.

"From when I was small, very small," Minerva's grandmother mumbles. "A story that my grandmother told *me*, about the ceibas of Chiapas. The sacred trees."

Minerva does not know this story. She feels her fingers trembling, but this time from something else, from some shred of a shred of an unnamed hope. She leans forward.

"When I was a child, I had terrible nightmares," her grandmother says, and Minerva cannot help but think of the dark beach, the tangled matrix of flesh and eyeballs. "I cried every night. So *my* grandmother, she made me a new pillow, using the cotton of the ceiba."

Minerva knows the tree, of course: an ecological linchpin of the Selva Lacandona, a beautiful hulking thing that can surpass forty meters, coated in spines and pink flowers. She knows its importance to the jungle and to the Maya who have lived there for thousands of years.

"My grandmother explained to me that the ceiba is a bridge, between this world and the other." She raises her gnarled hands, laces her fingers. "Entre el mundo y el inframundo. Xibalbá." She gives a watery laugh. "I knew nothing about Xibalbá. My father, he was so scared of brujas, so scared of hechizos. He never liked those stories. But my grandmother, when she brought me the new pillow, she sat by my bed and she told me."

Minerva sees an expression flash like sheet lightning across her grandmother's lined face, joy and anticipation, an echo of the child she was some eighty years ago.

"When the Catholic priests translated the Popol Vuh, they made Xibalbá into hell," she says. "It's true, my grandmother told me, that Xibalbá is a death place. A dark place. But after a day in the hot sun, she asked me, is there anywhere more welcoming than the shade?"

Minerva's grandmother becomes a child in the telling, and Minerva becomes one in the listening, swept away by the images: the four towering ceibas planted by the gods, one in each corner of the cosmos, thorny branches hung with Xtabay's would-be lovers, roots reaching so deep they pierce the barrier between living and dead.

The entrance to Xibalbá itself, a tangle of vines and night-blooming flowers, glowing with an unearthly luminescence, a multicolor mirror for the heavenly bodies moving far above. Through the portal: a city for the dead, but made of living wood and flowing water, cool and damp.

"After that night, I dreamed only of Xibalbá," she finishes. "With my pillow made of ceiba cotton. Even now, I think I believe more in Xibalbá than I do in heaven or hell." She sucks in a raspy breath. "Pero que cansada estoy."

Minerva emerges from the reverie. She can still hear the voice of her grandmother, and of her great-great-grandmother, moving through her blood. "Okay," she says, only half there. "Buenas noches, abuela."

"Buenas noches, nena," her grandmother says. "Te quiero tanto."

For the first time in months, she does not ask where Minerva is or when she is coming home. She reaches forward with a veiny hand and ends the call.

Minerva sits very still. Tears are collecting in the bottom of her goggles, fogging them. Tears of happiness, to see a grandmother so much closer to the one she remembers, and tears of misery, because she realizes she has been treating her grandmother like she is already dead. Preserved, entombed, untouchable.

In the lonely hospice quarantine, is it any wonder her grandmother retreats into her happy memories? With her aging brain starved for input, is it any wonder she whittles herself down to the same questions and answers?

Maybe the deviation tonight was a fluke, the vagaries of collapsing neurons. But maybe it was something else. Either way, Minerva sees now that she has been distancing herself, preparing herself, for a very long time—because she knows that when her grandmother dies, it will tear her in two.

She pulls the goggles from her face with a tear-slick pop. She cries for a while. Afterward she crawls into bed, wraps her arms around Ish, and whispers "Te quiero tanto" into the nape of his sunbrowned neck.

The days are hot and the sim grows fail, but the digivisits have changed.

Minerva does not try to burn away the fog the way she did that first night, but she does not sit in silence, nodding, humming. She prods at her grandmother, makes the jokes they used to make together. She presents the latest problems from the lab. She tells her about the lizards chasing one another in circles around the terrace, about the lotus bulb she bought in Xochimilco.

She is sifting for flint. Searching for sparks. Sometimes she sees it is tiring to her grandmother, feels guilty, and lets her retreat into the stories. But the stories have changed too: they are less and less about the pueblo, with its beautiful flowers and dirt streets, and more about the jungle, about the deep roots and deeper caves snaking downward toward Xibalbá.

It carries over into Minerva's dreams: no more drowning women, no more watchful monsters. Instead she dreams she is making a hole in the street with an electric drill, boring through the concrete to the underworld below. Molecular models drift up from the portal like phantoms, joining and breaking just beyond her fingertips.

Her grandmother tells her that Xibalbá is not a reward or a punishment, only part of a natural cycle that must be maintained. The rain falling, the sun rising, the stars moving—all cycles that were once maintained by sacrifice, which was not always the ugly fearful thing described by Catholic priests, any more than Xibalbá was always a place of torture and trickery.

The sim grows fail, but in more interesting ways. Every night Minerva's grandmother gives her benediction, tells her that the city of wood and water is coming, and Minerva cannot help but feel that she is right. That something ancient, something ancestral, has taken root not only in her grandmother but also in her.

Ish notices too. "You're sleeping better," he says one morning, over the bubble and sputter of the frying pan—eggs from the neighbor's hen, onion and jitomate from the hydrogarden. "I even heard you laughing."

"In my sleep?" Minerva demands, clattering plates out of the cupboard.

"It was terrifying at first," Ish admits. "But then I started laughing too."

Minerva laughs now, trying to remember the fractured dream: climbing an enormous flowering tree, pricking her hands on the thorns but feeling no pain. She shovels two bites of breakfast into her mouth, scooped steaming from the pan, then runs to get her goggles.

※

Ceiba pentandra was sequenced by machine learning years ago, one of a hundred species rendered down to its genetic code and evaluated for utility. But that was years ago, before recombination tech reached its current heights, and Minerva's lab has been focused on adaptable lianas, carbon-sucking mosses.

When she goes to access its simulated DNA, hers is not the only user icon on the file. The lab in Guatemala, in cloudy Kob'an, is already at work. She pulls up a call window, sees Eduardo, one of her collaborators, with dark rings under his eyes but a gleam inside them. They speak over each other, but she knows they have dreamed the same dream.

The lab in Belize joins them a moment later: Celeste, the youngest biotech on the project, still tying up her jet-black curls. The three of them coordinate their efforts, sectioning up the code, hunting for the gene or genes they saw in the inframundo. Kike is already feeding possibilities into the sim queue.

Minerva works until her eyeballs ache and her eyelids scrape. Sometimes Ish pushes a glass of water into her hand, a thoughtful phantom in the void beyond her goggles. Sometimes she stretches her legs under the table, feels the flex of far-off tendons. Most often she is still as a rooted tree, only her eyes moving. She turns off all exterior notifications.

When the key arrives, a snippet of genetic material buried deep, a tiny unexpressed fragment of the ceiba's long history,

Minerva recognizes it like family. So do the others; they all three highlight it in nearly the same instant. They clear the sim queue, request processing power. They watch the sim grow begin.

It's close to midnight when Minerva finally pulls off her goggles. Ish is slumped snoring across from her, head nesting in his folded arms. "It's going to work," she says, and the words are stones lifted from her chest. "We'll need to make tweaks. We'll need to run more sims. But it's going to work."

Ish only drools, but she doesn't mind. There is someone else she wants to tell. She can stand the goggles a few minutes more; she is reaching to put them back on, to call her grandmother, when she sees her thumbnail screen is acid yellow. The message is not from the lab.

Her stomach plunges. She calls, and the hospice nurse answers. Explanation washes over her and only a few words emerge intact: arterial blockage, successive strokes, the second fatal. Her grandmother's vitals had been so steady for so many weeks. So steady Minerva thought nothing of switching off notifications.

"She was conscious for a few moments in between," the nurse says. "She asked where she was, and when she was going home." He pauses. "And then she said Xibalbá was calling. Nos vemos en noviembre."

Minerva pulls the goggles off, and weeps.

It's Día de Muertos, and Minerva is up on the terrace. The ocher sky is darkening, billowing clouds illuminated by jags of distant lightning. She leans back in her chair and puts her feet on the other, head tipped back to watch. It used to feel like life or death, waiting for the clouds to buckle and split, waiting for the first droplet of rain.

But that was the old days, before sim grows became reality and Xibalbá—there could be no other name for the plant, the nanobionic hybrid of artificial genes and ancient ones—took root. Now the garden is flourishing and the hydroponic systems are quaint, antiquated.

Her guava trees grow from the concrete, fed by Xibalbá's omnipresent filament web. Her orchids and mala madres explode from the walls in a beautiful chaos. And when she turns her head to look over the edge of the terrace, she sees the city her great-great-grandmother dreamed of.

Xibalbá snakes through every cubic meter of concrete, coats it with dark green tendrils. It bears little resemblance to the ceiba that completed its genetic code. No sharp spines, no seedpods full of cotton. But it has something even better, a final tweak that was not strictly necessary for its success.

"Ready to go?" Ish asks, appearing at the top of the vine-wreathed metal staircase, sleek white skull mask in hand. He holds it in front of his face. "No more work today. Parties only."

Down below, the party is in full swing. The streets are pulsing with music and laughter, costumed revelers trickling back from the parade, mingling with their families. Most of the decorations are unchanged, but the strings of LED bulbs are no more. Instead, sprouting from the vine-swathed street lamps, from the overgrown skyscrapers, bioluminescent flowers of every conceivable color bloom through the dark.

For tonight, the whole of Mexico City is her grandmother's ofrenda. But she made a smaller one, too, downstairs, and snipped the very brightest flowers from the verbena to lay across it. She takes a deep breath, inhaling the cool floral air, picturing the childish joy that must be on her grandmother's face even now. For a moment, everything is still and perfectly preserved.

"Ready," she says, and rejoins the cycle.

Accensa Domo Proximi

Cameron Nell Ishee

It was a typical Thursday, except for the potatoes. Dario and Vin stared down at the heap of them: crispy hash browns here, grilled home fries there. A half dozen peeled spuds sat in a bucket of cold water, waiting for a turn that wouldn't come.

"Huh," Vin said.

"Huh," Dario agreed.

"I don't think this has ever happened before," Vin commented.

"Not while I've worked here," Dario concurred.

"So what do we do with . . ." Vin's gesture was a little helpless, a half-limp sweep of the sheer volume of uneaten potatoes in the kitchen.

Zinnia poked her head in from the front-of-house. "Honestly," she said. "Am I going to have to come back there? It's turnover in, like, twenty minutes."

"Nobody ordered potatoes," Dario told her. "Like, at all. All day."

"No fries," Vin said.

"No hash browns," Dario said.

"No baked," Vin added.

"No roasted," Dario said, starting to smile.

"No scalloped."

"No mashed."

"No chips."

Dario grinned. "Ooh, good one. Here: no *latkes*."

"Damn!" Vin said. "No gnocchi."

"No gratin."

"No salad."

"No hasseltop," Dario said, and Zinnia clapped her hands to get their attention.

"It's hassel*back*, children! Seriously, how are you cooks?"

Vin flicked a fry at her. "Pretty sure we're both older than you, fingerling." He threw a fry at Dario, who caught it in his mouth.

"No fingerlings!" Dario said around the fry. It was salty and perfect.

"Half that stuff's not even on the menu. We can leave it for the Lux," Zinnia said, but she sidled over to shovel fries into the prodigious takeout pouch on her purse.

"The Lux don't do potatoes," Vin said.

"*Nothing* potato?" Dario asked, incredulous.

Vin popped his shoulders up and down, then pulled out his phone. "Maybe Jay can pull a special out of the ones we peeled, but those already breakfast-ified will have to come with us."

"Well, get to packing up," Zinnia said. "I wasn't kidding about turnover. We gotta hustle. You need me to help clean up back here?"

Dario shook his head. "We *need* you to de-potato us," he said. "We prepped everything, like normal."

"Didn't know it was gonna be No-Potato Thursday," Vin said, tossing Dario another fry.

"Didn't know it was Spud Sunday," Dario said.

Vin snorted, but he was already getting the prepared food stowed in to-go boxes. "How does that one make sense?"

"Day of rest, right?" Dario said. "But, like, for potatoes."

"Y'all gonna be on a permanent rest if the B team gets here and the kitchen's not nice and shiny for them," Zinnia said.

Dario just laughed, though he did start collecting utensils to stick in the sanitizer. "I'll tell Jay you called them the B team, and we'll see about that permanent rest," he said. When she kept hovering, he realized she was actually concerned and changed his tack. "Look, we're all good back here. Just swap the signs out front and take as many potatoes as you can on the way out. We'll be done in no time."

He was telling the truth: fifteen minutes later, the three of them were standing on the platform in front of the little restaurant, balancing cartons of potatoes underneath the repixelating sign. Their sluggish system was at least ten years old, and it took a good while for Amazing Audrey's Eggs-a-Plenty to shift over to the Luxembourg. Once the algorithm got out of bed, though, it would scrub over everything. Double-A's had tile, while the Lux favored wood paneling. Yellow and white would be replaced by blue and brown, and the kitschy chicken paintings would flip around to black-and-white landscape photography.

Dario had seen places that had even more settings, and though he didn't spend much time in the hyperwired underground, he'd heard there were eateries that could microcustomize down to the level of the individual table.

He toggled on their bullshit security system, mostly out of

habit, and went to wait for the Leveler with the others. They were sitting out of the sun beneath the station overhang.

"I mean, I just don't get pings from *dudes in the park*," Vin was teasing.

"Shows what you know." Zinnia sniffed. "Yeong-cheol Min? Seriously? No name recognition there at all?"

Vin leaned around Zinnia to loop Dario in. "She says there's an old dude gonna be in KSW Memorial. He pinged her."

"The Arts in the Park people pinged me," Zinnia corrected. "I subscribe because I'm not an uncultured plebeian."

"We're plebs," Vin said with mock sadness.

"Pleb," Dario agreed.

Zinnia continued as if they hadn't interrupted, which, in Dario's opinion, was a fairly sound strategy. "Yeong-cheol Min is, like, *the* greatest living artist of our time, at least in the field of pottery. It's day four of his live performance."

The Leveler pulled up, all shiny chrome and green plastic, and they jostled into a compartment. "So," Dario said, "we're going to KSW Memorial? For pottery? How do you even do a *live show* for pottery?"

"He takes it out of the ground," Zinnia informed them. She paused for a second, while the automated voice reminded them to keep their limbs inside the compartment while the Leveler was in motion and not to forget their stop. Then she continued: "Day one, he digs up a bunch of dirt and extracts the clay."

"I thought you needed special dirt for pottery," Dario commented. "Special pottery clay or whatever."

Vin shook his head. "No, there's at least a little clay in most soils. You never did that in fourth grade? Filter out the clay, make your own little pinch pots? That's like, a right of passage, man. I mean, were you even a nine-year-old if you didn't make a pinch pot in art class?"

"It didn't come up," Dario said, a little shorter than he meant it. He rearranged the cartons of potatoes in his arms, partly so he wouldn't have to see their faces when they remembered.

"Oh," Vin said, abashed. "Yeah, sorry, right, I mean—"

He shut up abruptly, and Dario shot Zinnia an appreciative look, knowing she was somehow behind it. She was safer to look at, just then; he doubted she had the capacity to pity him. Compassion, maybe. But pity? He couldn't even picture it on her face.

She was poised as ever. "The first day, he digs up the dirt. Has to get a permit for it, but who's gonna deny *Yeong-cheol Min* a permit? Besides, he puts almost all of it back—just keeps the extracted clay. Then, it's got to sit for a while. Day two, he refines it some more. There's stuff you have to do, to remove air bubbles and other impurities that could break the work once it's fired. But then he starts working it, and that's the really cool bit. Usually, he finishes in a day, but this one is *huge*. My feed is full of pictures, but I can't tell what it is."

Vin asked, "So he's finishing it today? Or still shaping?"

"Still shaping," Zinnia said. "Maybe he'll finish today, maybe he won't. That's part of what's so exciting!"

"And we're bringing a butt-ton of potatoes to this event because . . . ?" Dario inquired. "I mean, not that I was doing anything else this afternoon. But still. How is this your solution to the inexplicable potato event?"

"IPE for short," Vin put in. "It needs an acronym."

"So we can eat while we watch the pottery performance," Zinnia said, as though this were obvious. "And, like, give potatoes away. To whoever."

Vin and Dario exchanged a look. Vin's wide eyes said, *It's too precious, I can't even try.* The quirk of Dario's mouth said, *We're not horrible enough to tease her over this.* Silently, they agreed. Privately, Dario knew they were both going to ping Jay about this later.

"Sounds like a great plan, Zin," Vin said. He got one of her to-go boxes added to his pile for his trouble.

"Thanks for the support, Vinnia," Zinnia said, and they lapsed into companionable public transit silence.

In Dario's opinion, the Leveler was misnamed. Sure, it moved up and down between the various vertical levels of the city, but it also ran on a lateral route. *Like a train*, he thought. *Or an elevator. A trainevator.*

"Trainevator," he said out loud.

Vin's eyes lit up. "Eletrain," he said.

"Escalatrain."

"Escala*tram*," Vin shot back, and Zinnia groaned and put on her headphones for the remainder of the trip.

Ken Saro-Wiwa Memorial Park was several levels down and many blocks over from Double-A's. They usually finished up with the late brunch crowd just in time to meet the transit rush of kids getting out of school, and this day was no exception in that regard. By the time they actually made it to the park, they'd successfully redistributed nearly a third of the potatoes.

"Hop the Parkline?" Vin suggested as they exited the Leveler.

"Nah," Dario said. "I feel like walking. Been standing at the griddle all morning."

Zinnia guided them in the general direction of the art event, and a part of Dario relaxed as soon as they were under the leafy canopy. The temperature dropped immediately in this shade, and the cool of it was soothing. Bushy oaks lined every walking path, the Parkline winding unobtrusively between them.

His childhood home had had trees like this, before, though those oaks had been bendier and lichen draped. It had been the salt that killed them even before the water, and he'd grieved them with the passion a small child can muster for such an occasion. This city was verdant, an intentionality that drew him here in the first place when he had to be resettled. But a place like this, heavy with oaks, would always speak to him in a way the vine-covered buildings and succulent-lined sidewalks just didn't.

When they saw the crowd, Dario's first thought was, *Huh, I guess people* do *turn out for a live pottery show.*

"I'm impressed," Vin said, echoing Dario's own thoughts.

"Told you," Zinnia sang. "This is a big deal!"

Dario had never been to this corner of the park before. The ground sloped down into a sort of naturalistic amphitheater full of people. The landscape created a hole in the tree cover, and the midafternoon sun poured down on the spectacle in the middle: an older man, graying hair pulled back in a scraggly ponytail, arranging heaps of reddish mud.

Dario's first impression of Yeong-cheol Min was, *I wouldn't recognize him on the street.* The artist was unobtrusive, his features unremarkable and his presentation lacking ostentation. He could have been any of the grandfathers who sat outside their doors on Dario's street, gossiping among one another. He wore much-stained denim overalls and a short-sleeved shirt gone grayish red from his work, and as Dario watched, he rolled the side of his own pant leg over a patch of clay, leaving behind the texture of the cloth.

"I don't know what I was expecting," Dario said aloud. "This all seems pretty chill."

The crowd around them was buzzing with the low undercurrent

of conversation, and that made the scene even more approachable. The three of them picked their way through the assembled people, offering potatoes to strangers until they were left with just one container each and had arrived at a good spot to watch.

The grassy ground gave under Dario's feet just slightly as he shifted his weight. Vin held up his to-go plate, and Dario helped him split their food so that they'd have an equal amount of hash browns and fries. Zinnia carried two types of hot sauce with her at all times, and they took a moment to bicker over which one was better. Then, as they ate, Dario turned his attention back to the live performance.

It was hard to assess what exactly the artist was making, but Dario wasn't quite ready to call it abstract. The curved spires and chunky blocks seemed familiar somehow, in a way he couldn't put his finger on. Staring at it was like getting the ghost of a tune caught in his head, too small a scrap to look up. In such a case, he was relegated to humming it under his breath, hoping to eventually chance upon a lyric somewhere in the crevices of his mind.

Yeong-cheol periodically returned to a box of tools, which he employed to texture the clay in places. There were sharp sticks, scalpels for carving, and little wheels for adding tracks. Then, there was the artist's own body: He rubbed his hands over the clay, sometimes dipping them in water. He turned the side of his head against a section, printing the clay with little lines from his hair. Gently, ever so gently, he brought his bare feet up to the work and squished the clay between his toes.

The familiarity of it was getting to Dario in a way he couldn't express. *I know this. How do I know this?* He couldn't recall having so much as heard of this artist before, much less seen his work. And, as he'd told the others, Dario had not had the kind of childhood where one was taught to play with clay. There was no obvious reason for this feeling in his chest, and he tried to push it away.

In front of the patch of grass that Dario, Vin, and Zinnia had staked out, an older woman sat in rapture. Dario watched her watch Yeong-cheol and was more than a little disturbed to see tears tracking down her face. The most unsettling thing was, he could feel the tightness in his own chest too. He didn't want it, couldn't understand it.

This is a goddamn live pottery show, he chided himself. *What is so upsetting about it? There's nothing wrong here, nothing bad. What's going on?*

He turned to his friends, but they seemed unaffected by whatever was taking place. Zinnia was taking pictures, swiping through different filters. Vin was about as interested in the potatoes as he was in the artwork unfolding before him.

Dario watched for a good ten minutes before he put it together: Yeong-cheol added a lump of clay, sticking it onto a wire in such a way that it might balance at a precarious angle. Then, he added another. And another.

Archipelago. The word popped into Dario's mind, and he course-corrected immediately. *No. Barrier islands.* He realized that he was looking at a stylized depiction of a coastline. *His* coastline. Before.

He could name them from their shape as they appeared under Yeong-cheol's hands: *Cat Island. Ship Island. Horn, Petit Bois, Dauphin.*

His breath caught in his throat, and the names came fast as he raked his gaze over the work, this time seeing it for what it was. *Mobile Bay to the east, Lake Pontchartrain to the west. On one side, the Pascagoula River, curving around Moss Point. On the other side, Bay St. Louis, ringed by Henderson Point, Pass Christian, DeLisle.*

Dario's eyes tracked the snarl of the Wolf River, then drifted over, almost against his will, to the looping tangle of earth and water that was where the Biloxi met the sea. In this work of art, the land was still land, worked in clay, but the water was represented by air. An absence. Not the presence that had risen, consumed.

Old Fort—we used to hunt for frogs. Davis Bayou. He watched Yeong-cheol shape Deer Island across the mouth of the bay, and inside his shoes he flexed his toes, remembering the sand. *Why is he doing this? How does he know?*

It occurred to Dario that there were maps, that the artist could have consulted records to know this place that was. He looked for, and found, the little inlet where he'd grown up. *Halstead Bayou.* It would have been easy to miss, easy to exclude. A sliver of a place, an intertidal zone at the end of the world. Long since swallowed by the insistent sea, little by little and then all at once, in a storm so great it decimated the very ground they might have rebuilt on. A shadow of Dario's life was still there, a heat haze of childhood memories buried in sand and rubble and water.

The water, the water, the water. His aunt used to say, "It giveth and it taketh away," but Dario had hated that. It spoke to an undulation where he'd only experienced an escalation. It implied a reciprocity that he didn't think had been present for a very, very long time before the end.

"I think it's some type of crown," Zinnia said. "If you cut a crown, and unwrapped it, like. You know?"

"Nah, I think it's supposed to be mountains," Vin said. "See all the pointy parts? And the wavy bits, that's, like, where the rivers come down in between. You see it?"

Dario didn't correct them. He didn't want to explain, didn't want to verbalize what he was feeling just yet. He wasn't crying, but now he looked at the old woman in front of them and thought he saw the echoes of his own family in her grief-stricken face. His grandmother had always kept her composure, at least in front of the kids. He wondered if this is what she might have looked like, in the absence of her family's confining, bracing weight.

He didn't know how long they watched. Long enough that Zinnia started messaging with a friend, on one side of him. Long enough that Vin got distracted, feeding little bits of potato to the ants, on the other side of him. But Dario watched, and watched, and watched. Under Yeong-cheol's hands, the world was recreated. Dario could feel the echo of mud under his own fingernails—he'd been young enough that digging through rubble was a treasure hunt on par with catching crabs, the thrill of discovery muddled in with a baseline horror not quite over his head.

Toward the end—Dario knew it was the end, could sense the completeness of it—the old man took a sharp stick. Across the bottom, he carved the words *Accensa Domo Proximi*.

"Ooh," Zinnia said beside him, typing furiously with her thumbs. "Okay, okay. I'm on Grapevine, and people are posting that it's a map or something. And that would be Latin, right? Did either of you take Latin in school?"

Dario ignored her and found himself moving through the crowd, to the very front. There was no barrier separating the artist and the assembled, the work from its watchers. He simply stepped through the people, across the short, empty space they'd left by popular consensus, and found himself inches from the enormous clay representation.

Slowly, carefully, he reached out. Dario rolled the pad of his thumb over the spot where Halstead Bayou used to be, leaving behind a faint ridged whorl. Then he stepped back, all too aware of the escalating volume of the crowd and the number of cameras that were now pointed at him.

He met Yeong-cheol's eyes, not knowing what to expect. But there was understanding there, and he came over to inspect the small mark Dario had made. "This is good, I think," he said, speaking for the first time. His English had a very slight British accent to it. "Ocean Springs?"

"Yes," Dario said, still unsure. His thoughts were starting to catch up to him: *You touched it. One of the greatest living artists, Zinnia said! What are you doing? How could you—*

"I'm from the coast too," Yeong-cheol said, nodding. "An island that is no more. I've done several versions of it by now. The best one is on exhibit in Seoul. This is my first attempt at your home, however. How do you think I did?"

"I recognize it," Dario managed. He hadn't called it home in a long time. "All of it."

For some reason, that made the old man smile. "Good. I'm leaving it here, you know. A permanent installation, once it is properly fired. You can come visit whenever you want." He pointed to the thumbprint and said, "This, in particular, will make it memorable. I think we keep it, don't you?"

Dario nodded. He would have nodded no matter what Yeong-cheol said, but now he felt an odd sort of relief bloom in his chest. He met the man's eyes again and saw that same understanding, even as his own thoughts came disjointed. *What it's like. When the death of your home is someone else's lesson learned.* That was by far the most grating thing about this city, for all its solar panels and biodegradable take-out boxes. He'd never been to a single memorial, even though they held them every year. A few speeches couldn't hold the depths of the loss between their meager words, couldn't scrape together the brokenness that had wracked that land long before the salt water, and he'd always been uninterested in listening to people flail as they tried to do it justice aloud.

This, though? All the maps he'd ever seen had been oriented north-south, with these places on the periphery. But this representation arranged it the other way, as if the ground beneath it was the main of the continent, the features emerging up into the air at eye level as the focus.

Dario stepped back, and back again, and suddenly Zinnia and Vin were at his side. A quick glance at their resolve told him that they might not have understood what was going on, but they were ready to back him up anyway. The flowers of relief under his skin pulled at him, turned toward the warmth of their affection.

Yeong-cheol addressed the crowd, even as he dipped his hands into a new bucket and came out with a white, viscous substance. "Accensa domo proximi, tua quoque periclitatur," he said as he began to gently coat the statue. "It's unattributed, but a powerful line. 'When the house of your neighbor burns, your own home is likewise in danger.' A millennia-old phrase, passed down through generations. And yet not something our collective human society managed to internalize, at least in certain arenas, until recently. So now, I show you: it burns."

He produced a lighter—an old-fashioned one that clicked as he sparked it to life. Then, he touched it to the corner of the statue, and the white liquid caught, turning flame blue.

Some people cried out, and most everyone stepped back from the sudden heat of it. But Dario stayed put and closed his eyes. He felt the warmth on his face, on his bare arms. His friends pressed up against him on either side, but they didn't retreat.

The moment lasted for a long, long time. When he finally opened his eyes, the structure before him still glowed blue.

"The firing," Zinnia said, unusually subdued beside him. "It'll go on for the better part of the night. You want to stay and watch?"

Dario thought about it. He rubbed the barest bit of clay residue between his thumb and forefinger and took in the feeling of it, paired with the feeling of being among this crowd. Watching the sculpture with all of them felt a little like it wasn't just *his*, like they were carrying this together. "Yeah," he said and finally retreated to a more comfortable distance. He sat, and his friends joined him. "Yeah, I think I do."

Cabbage Koora: A Prognostic Autobiography

Sanjana Sekhar

Thursday, February 9, 2023

I'm bundled in a wool overcoat against the 6:00 a.m. winter chill of Los Angeles. The former New Yorker in me scoffs at how soft I've become against the cold—or rather, the "cold," since it's a full fifty degrees and I'm shivering. Today's high is eighty, so by noon I'll have stripped down to a crop top. I know it's climate change and all, but I'd be lying if I said I'm not just a tiny bit excited for a short reprieve from the monotonous months of fifty degrees and rainy that we've been having this winter.

The morning frost on my Subaru is tenacious, even after I run the engine for a little while. I'm bordering on late for kathak class, so I pull out of the driveway with icy windows and hurry to beat the rush hour traffic.

In the studio it's a steady thrum of the tabla over the stereo system:

tha ki ta tha ki ta—gin na
tha ki ta tha ki ta—gin na
tha ki ta tha ki ta—gin na—dha
                    gin na—dha
                    gin na—dha

And then a relentlessly driving pace of *chakkar*, or one-count spins:

tig dha dig dig ek . . .
                do . . .
                teen . . .
                chaar . . .
                paanch . . .
                chhe . . .
                saath . . .

And on and on.

After an hour of this, I'm breathless. We've been drilling a composition with thirty-one *chakkar*, and even after months, I'm losing my balance somewhere around twenty-six.

I leave class and head back to my car, protein shake in hand, sweat gluing my kurta to my skin, a string of profanities running through my mind as I scold myself for tapping out at twenty-six. I've just slipped into my driver's seat when my phone rings. One peek at the screen and my mood elevates.

"Hi, Amma," I say with unrestrained fondness as my mother's face grins back at me over FaceTime.

"Hi, *chinna*," she responds with equal affection. "Just finished kathak?"

"Yeah, about to head to the grocery store on my way home."

"Shall we quickly call Ammamma before she sleeps?"

"Sure. My parking meter's out in ten, though."

"We can just say hi. FaceTime or WhatsApp?"

"FaceTime. Can you add her in?"

"One minute."

After some shuffling around, a second little box populates on my screen, offering me the stray wisps of white hair otherwise known as the top of my grandmother's head.

"Hi, Ammamma," I say.

"Hi, Amma," my mom chirps.

"Hi, *kanna. Bujie kanna re.* Sweetie *kanna*," my ammamma's forehead croons. "How are you both?"

"Good. Can you bring the phone down?" I say, holding back a laugh. "We only see the top of your head."

Amma and I call Ammamma together every week. It used to be Sundays, like clockwork, when I was in grade school. Now it's sort of whenever we catch each other. Every week we remind her to tilt the phone down so we can actually see her face. And every week she insists on greeting us with her forehead.

Ammamma's puttering around her kitchen in Hyderabad, 8,711 miles away from me in California. My memory conjures up the smell of hearty *palakura pappu* and fluffy *idli*. Chili-spiced *toor dal* roasting on the *tava* for homemade *podi*. The softness of her orange sari, *pallu* tied securely around her waist so it stays out of the way of her busy hands.

She's lived alone in Tarnaka for almost forty years, ever since my grandfather passed away. She's eighty-five now and wobbles about her small flat with the vigor and determined independence of a twenty-year-old. My amma got this from her, I think. I swear my amma will be single-handedly shoveling piles of snow as tall as she is (five whole feet) from her Park City, Utah, driveway until she's ninety years old.

I tell Ammamma about kathak class, and she glows with pride. "Very good, *kanna.* Very good. I'm very glad you're keeping up with kathak. Very good."

"I'll show you this new composition when I next come, Ammamma." She smiles the most when I promise this. Every year, when we visit her in India, I dance for her. In those fifteen minutes while she watches, she's filled with more childlike joy, more wonder, more freedom of spirit, than any other moment I see her. My grandma, like many women in her generation, carries a deep anxiety. Kathak transcends that, transports us together, unlocks her. Dance is hardly my profession, but it has a cemented place in my life as a psychosomatic way to stay rooted in culture and family from half a world away. As a way of staying connected to Ammamma.

"*Aim chestunavu*, Amma? What are you doing?" my mom asks her mother.

"*Aim ledu.* Just putting away the food."

"What did you make for dinner?"

"Nothing much," Ammamma says. "Some *pappannam*, that is all. Tomorrow I'll make some cabbage *koora.*" She pauses in her puttering to pick up something off the counter. "See? Do you see the cabbage?"

Ammamma adjusts the angle of the camera in an effort to show us her cabbage. "Do you see?" But she's pointing the camera at her ceiling, and I'm having a hard time repressing my laughter.

"No, Ammamma, we can't see. You're showing us the ceiling."

Ammamma adjusts the angle again, and now we're feasting our eyes on a sliver of her ceiling that's been joined by a section of her wall.

"Now? Now do you see? Do you see the cabbage?"

Amma is openly laughing. "No, Ma, we don't see the cabbage. You're showing the wall."

Another unsuccessful adjustment, then: "Okay, now? Now do you see the cabbage? Do you see the cabbage?"

Ammamma's excitement is only intensifying, but no cabbage has made an appearance thus far. Now Amma and I are both shaking with mirth.

"Do you see it?" Ammamma continues to insist.

We don't answer because we're too busy gasping for breath. Then, miraculously, we see a sliver of a blurry green leaf flash across her FaceTime camera.

"Oh!" Amma and I both shout.

"We see it, Ammamma!"

"Yes, yes, we see it, Ma."

"You see the cabbage? You see it?"

"Yes! Yes, Ammamma, we see the cabbage!"

Now even Ammamma is laughing.

I screenshot this moment several times, never wanting to forget these small winks of diasporic joy, the three of us spread across three cities and three generations, giggling like sisters together on a sunshine summer afternoon.

It's not long before Ammamma's chuckles turn into coughs, peppered by a sort of rough wheezing that I learned as a child is part of her chronic asthma. My parking meter blinks red.

Tuesday, November 19, 2047

I'm in the front yard, doling out carefully measured sprinkles of water to the small garden I've struggled to nurture for the last several growing seasons. The water rations for victory gardens have gotten more and more economical over the last ten years.

In our little patch we still get tomatoes and kale and grow some neem, and the occasional surprise potatoes spring out from wherever we've last dug in compost. The rest of our food comes from the community garden (which does better some years than others), the local co-op (which is not always well stocked because it hasn't quite yet reached financial stability), or with great burden to our wallets (anything requiring long-distance freight costs an arm and a leg now, partially because it's just too expensive at a basic resource and carbon level, and partially because of the taxes they've been trying to institute on nonlocal food).

It's been a tough transition period. Here in California, we have the farming infrastructure but not the water. In other parts of the country, land that's been monocropped under generations of agribusiness is in various stages of transition to regenerative farming. The question of who pays for this transition, what carbon taxes get charged or credited and to whom, and who leads the proposed solutions that take the place of the old order . . . Well, it's been a thorny time. But it's also a time of inspired experimentation. I remind myself of that when the overwhelm hits. I remind myself of the energy.

Where we live, in the historically Black neighborhood of Leimert Park, our family's borne witness and offered support as those who've been holding it down here for generations lead the charge on collective care: with community gardens, co-ops, free fridges, heat shelters, communal front yard victory gardens, shade tree planting, seed saving, after-school programs, "Buy Nothing" gift economy groups, car shares, and so much more. Funding is a constant issue for these initiatives (right now the biggest source of funding is private donors, but the community is keenly problem-solving for a self-sufficient model). Everything's decided at our monthly town hall meetings, which are always lively and full of opinions. There's a small group of us South Asians in the neighborhood, and our agreed-upon job at these meetings is mostly to listen well and provide the chai.

Out in the garden, dusk is dancing vividly before me, blues chasing pinks chasing oranges across the hazy horizon. I always stop to cherish it, never knowing how many more I'll savor before the smog swallows up color altogether.

I pause over the far end of the garden, which has been exceptionally dry no matter how much I try to feed it. It's honestly a little embarrassing. My neighbors' victory gardens look far more luscious than mine. The community decided at one of our first meetings years ago that victory gardens would go in the front yard (communal, conversational, open, and engaging) rather than in the backyard (hidden, private, inaccessible). Ninety-nine percent of the time, I love that we made this decision. The 1 percent is just the occasional despair I feel when I remember that my garden is on display and not in the best shape, and my ego gets to me. I make a mental note to hop next door tomorrow to Amrit and Hari's to ask Hari what cover crops are working in his yard these days—his green thumb has always guided mine, and maybe he'll know how to better nourish this dry patch.

From somewhere inside the house, my phone rings.

"Amma!" Gita calls to me. "It's Ammamma."

Her five-foot frame, identical to mine, comes bounding through the open screen door, my phone in her hand.

Gita's hair is curly like mine, and I fucking love that about her. She's smart as a whip, and I love that even more about her. Sometimes I look at her and marvel at the fact that I *made* that creature. Now I understand what my amma means when she says "Having a kid is like putting your heart outside of yourself and watching it walk around," or some shit like that. Sometimes I want to gather Gita up and store her safely back inside my body.

She comes over to me and scoops me into an affectionate hug before setting the phone up flat on the porch table and hitting "answer." We both activate the bracelets on our wrists. Almost immediately a spark of light projects upward from the Beam projection port on my phone, and a three-dimensional hologram of my mother takes shape from the light.

"Hi Amma," I say.

"Hi Ammamma!" Gita says brightly.

"Hello? Hello?" my mom says. "I can't see you."

No matter how many times we do this, she always comes in perplexed at the beginning of a Beam call.

"Amma, did you put it face down on the table again?"

"*Allari pilla!* Troublemaker. I kept it properly face up. I'm not that technologically challenged. But still I don't see you."

"Did you turn the brightness back up, or is it in night mode?"

"Oh. One minute. How do I do that again?"

"There's a control on your bracelet. This is why I was saying you should just leave it on the automatic setting."

"I can figure it out. I don't like how bright it is on auto—it makes my eyes burn."

We watch her hologram-self fidget with something off camera, before she lights up in delight.

"Got it!" she says. "Hi! Oh, Gita you're looking so nice. Are you going somewhere?"

"Thanks, Ammamma," Gita says. "I was invited to a prayer circle tonight, in preparation for the burns next week. Elena is leading, and she told me I could bring some jasmine and *haldi* and *chandan* as offerings from our family."

For the past few years, Gita's been volunteering with the Tongva Conservancy's ceremonial burns, covering any responsibilities she's invited to participate in. Fire season has worsened over the last ten years in California, so many regions, including Los Angeles County, realized survival depended on working with local tribes to revive cultural burning practices. The prescribed burns that Indigenous folks across the world have practiced culturally since time immemorial kept rampant dry brush under control and created a cycle of nourishment for the forests until colonialism outlawed the practice. In LA, the late fall burning they've restarted allows for plant life to rejuvenate in the rainy winter season, the goal being to once again transform dry underbrush into verdant vegetation come spring.

"How are you going there?" my amma asks Gita. "I thought your driving permits are Monday, Wednesday, Saturday?"

"Elena got a Tuesday slot in the community car share, so she's coming to pick me up. I think she got one of those Rivian two-doors!"

"Fancy," I say.

Gita goes inside to start gathering her things while I ask Amma what she's up to.

"Not much," Amma replies. "Just making your ammamma's cabbage *koora*."

"Tease!" I accuse.

"I sent you seeds last year!" Amma says defensively.

"Yeah, yeah, but they don't grow, I told you. The water they need is way beyond our rations."

We bicker warmly about cabbage—a nostalgic but water-intensive vegetable I probably haven't eaten in fifteen years at this point. As the cool night air sets in, Amma's hologram shines brightly above the porch table. A few stray moths, confused, start circling in the vicinity. I watch their wings disturb the pixels here and there.

When Elena's car (indeed a Rivian two-door) pulls up, Gita flashes by me with a kiss and hops in, leaving the divine aroma of jasmine and *chandan* in her wake. At the same moment, a second set of footsteps tip-tap up the stairs from the street into our garden, and I'm engulfed in a familiar embrace.

"Hi, buddy!" a voice coos at me. It's Aditi, close friend and coconspirator. She plops her bike helmet and backpack onto a chair on our porch. Seeing that my mom's on Beam on the table, she grins. "Hi, Aunty!" She hits the "join" button on her Beam bracelet so my mom can see her hologram, then sprawls out in the grass beside me. "How are you?"

"Hi, Aditi! Good, good. How are you? How's Noor?"

"They're good; they're still at the courthouse, or they would've come by with me." Then Aditi nods at her backpack and looks at me conspiratorially. "I went to the Indian store today."

I let out a whoop. This is a luxury we reserve only for special occasions. "Shut up. What're we celebrating?"

"Wellll, Noor Beamed me from the courthouse today and told me that our permit request for the collective is next in line for consideration. And that they think we're a sure thing."

Amma's hologram gasps. "The housing collective?"

"The one and only!" Aditi says.

That night, with Amma still on Beam, Aditi pulls out fresh guavas and late-season mangoes, a rare pleasure all the way from the subcontinent, and we twirl around . . .

tha ki ta tha ki ta—gin na
tha ki ta tha ki ta—gin na
              . . . between bites of home.

Friday, July 9, 2077

I eye the box on my coffee table with suspicion. Gita's had some strange contraption called *Iris* delivered to me, and she swears it's worth whatever trouble it surely brings. I asked Aditi and Noor about it, and they agreed that the concept of sticking digital contact lenses in one's eyes is unpleasant, to say the least. Gita has instructed me to be open to it and threatened to call me an old codger if I refuse to even try it out.

"Iris makes your eye a projector, Amma. Your *eye*. Can you believe it? It'll be like Reyna and I are there with you, 3D, walking and talking and interacting with you and your space. Like we're literally *there*," she said when we last talked.

The idea of feeling like my daughter and granddaughter are physically with me ultimately makes Iris an easy sell, despite my hesitations. Remembering her words, I decide to open the damn box.

After great difficulty and no small amount of grumbling, I've finally affixed the small translucent contacts to my eyes, and scrutinizing the user manual, I figure out how to power on this incredibly invasive piece of technology. I've had it on for less than two minutes when the accompanying earbud headphones inform me that I have an incoming call. It is, of course, Gita.

"Amma!" she shouts joyfully. "You did it! You finally listened to me! This is *so cool*."

I'm not sure exactly *what* is so cool, as my vision is blurry and I'm completely baffled by how she could possibly be seeing me right now. But I take her word for it. Gita does some troubleshooting that I don't understand, laughs at me quite a few times for being a bumbling fool with this new device, and finally coaches me through getting the focus in the lenses calibrated.

And then I see what's so cool. Gita has set it so that the simulated world we're in is my real front yard. I'm really here, right here, right now, lying in the grass. And it looks like they're here, too, as full-scale renderings of their real selves. They can interact with me, with my garden. On their end, Gita tells me, it's like being in virtual reality. She tells me that next time, we'll make the setting her house, where she and Reyna can move around in the real world and I'll be visiting via virtual reality. Once I've quit my grumblings, we settle into our regular pattern of conversation—what we're all eating, how everyone's love interests are, whether we're taking care of our health—except it *is* quite cool because the whole time it's like Gita and Reyna are lounging in the yard with me. I tell them this reminds me of way back when I was a kid in India, loitering outside all afternoon with my cousins.

"You used to go to India *every year*, Ammamma?" Reyna asks me, eyes wide.

"Every year. We were very lucky."

"Do you think you'll ever go back?"

"With the flight restrictions, it's almost impossible," I say. "Now I think it'd take me three trains and a whole-ass ship. No, I don't think I'll ever be able to go back. But sometime in the future . . . I think you will."

My girls both reach out to me as glittering pixels in the golden summer afternoon. I like how realistically Iris portrays them, truly as if they're here in the grass with me, just like Gita promised, reaching toward me to comfort me. But the technology misses what I love most about them: their smell, the warmth of their skin, the calm in my own heart when I'm in their physical presence.

When Gita told me she and her partner, Gloria, had decided to move away from LA to raise Reyna somewhere that was more climate stable, I understood. My mother left her mother in India to come to America in search of a better life, an economically stable life, a life that would offer the opportunity of abundance for us—for me—after the literal and metaphorical scarcity that British colonialism imposed on the subcontinent. At the time, who would've thought that decades later, rampant consumption and capitalism would finally deliver that same scarcity here to our doorsteps in America?

Then I moved away from my mother, starting a life in LA in community with other South Asian storytellers who were committed to drawing attention to climate and culture. Those of us who'd joined the movement as soon as we became conscious of it saw the writing on the wall long back, but it took the bubble actually popping around the wealthy for those in power to take any real action on what was going on.

In LA, most of the mansions in the hills got wiped out by fires long ago. A staccato of winter storms caused irreparable mudslides along Mulholland Drive. The Pacific Ocean claimed Santa Monica. The city was forced to implement retreat strategies, which led to them regulating lot sizes as more people had to relocate to the livable areas of LA. Predictably, some millionaires really fought against this and did everything they could to rebuild their mansions and add "climate-protective measures," but no one ever got too far in the process because insurance companies no longer covered houses built in long-designated Hazard Zones, and after a certain point, with all the carbon taxes levied on any building project that exceeded Reciprocal Resourcing Standards, the mansions were no longer financially viable. Other millionaires were shockingly supportive of the lot-size restrictions and wound up working within Reciprocal Resourcing Standards to build sustainable collectives.

Of course, some people still went the route of "save myself at the expense of others." They built bunkers with the goal of "self-sufficiency." It's a seductive idea, until you realize it means isolation from any sense of community. We are, by definition, interdependent. Our survival is predicated on our ability to work together. But I'm pretty sure Elon Musk's kids are still raising their families all alone in their secluded fortress. Their only outside interaction is probably with the drones that deliver their caviar.

Ultimately, it was the local resilience, the grassroots ideas, the place-based knowledge that allowed us to survive. These days, I live at Aunty Gang Collective (the name was inspired by Gita always calling me and my cherished group of South Asian women friends "Aunty Gang"). Here, there's no caviar (never understood the appeal, anyway), but there's music in the streets every day.

tha ki ta tha ki ta—gin na

After weathering a long waitlist at the permitting office, our little collective of fifteen homes was finally green-lit and built with reclaimed and organic material as part of a government-sponsored hyperlocalization effort. Over the last thirty years, LA was essentially renovated and rewilded by a team of what we would've called environmental architects back when I was growing up (today we just call them "architects"), led by a group of Indigenous engineers and designers.

We can't drive much anymore (even electric cars, which over time proved to be too resource intensive to continue manufacturing at scale), but it's okay because the electric buses and trains are much more connected than they used to be. Plus, Aditi and Noor are original Aunty Gang members and live just down the street. We hobble over to each other's houses almost every day.

"Okay, so India's off the table," Gita says, cutting off my thoughts, "but more realistically, can you come *here*, Amma? I told you, Gloria and I can arrange for the flight permits—we have so many credits from volunteer days with the ceremonial burning crews. The Aunty Gang can help you pack up, and you can be here by next week."

I make a face at her. I hope with Iris that she can properly see the extent of my disdain for this idea.

"Not this again, *kanna*." I stick her with an exaggerated eye roll. "Every call, the same thing: 'Amma, now that Dad has passed, what's left for you in LA? You're allllll aloooone, why don't you leave everything you've known for the last sixty years and come here to fucking Duluth, Minnesota, to join us in this commune of white people?' *Chhi!*"

"Well, it was either this or Vermont," Gita quips back. "And it's not called Duluth anymore. It's Onigamiinsing—it's Ojibwe. Anyway, please just think about it."

"I'll think about it," I lie.

"You say that every time, but you never really do."

"And yet you keep asking."

"I worry about you."

"And I worry about you, *kanna*."

"About me? I have Glo and Reyna. I don't like you being alone over there. You're eighty-two, and that's not young."

"Okay, first of all, *rude*. Second of all, I'm not alone! I have the Aunty Gang, all my friends within walking distance. The collective has grown a *lot* since you last visited. It's like a mini Wakanda here now. But with fewer beautiful superheroes and more elderly people."

"Waka-what?"

"Never mind, it was before your time. How's kathak class, Reyna?" I change the subject swiftly.

"Oh, good!" Reyna says. "We're working on *chakkar*. I'm up to thirty-one in a row! I can Iris you from our studio next time and show you, Ammamma. It'll be like you're watching me dance in person."

The thought fills me with pride. With longing. With wonder at the fact that so many generations, so many geographic locations and climate-related disruptions later, we preserve this art purely because it makes us happy.

"That would be lovely, *kanna*." I pause. "Actually, I wanted to show *you* something." I take a few steps over to my left. "Can you see?"

"See what? You'll have to be more specific, Amma," Gita says.

I point. "Okay, do you see this?" I'm gesturing to the front left corner of my garden, the dry section that insisted on following me from Leimert Park to Aunty Gang Co. The dry section where, years ago, I planted some cabbage seeds my mother had given me, though they never grew. The dry section that is now—

"I don't see where you're pointing, Amma," Gita says. "It must be out of scope. Let's expand the range on your Iris."

I fidget with the control she directs me toward.

"Okay, did it work?" I ask. "Can you see?"

Gita stifles a laugh and Reyna openly giggles. "No, Amma. I think you narrowed the scope."

"Oh. What do you see?"

"Your foot."

"Oops," I say. I try again, but the touchy control is so minimalist that I can't tell where on the range scale I am. "How about now? Now can you see it?"

"No, Ammamma," Reyna says with a laugh. "Now we see your left big toe. In *precise* detail."

I mumble some R-rated expletives under my breath. "But I can see you. How am I supposed to know what you're seeing? I told you I wouldn't like this Iris thing."

"Okay, let's stay calm," Gita says, still chuckling. She talks me through the bewildering device, and finally, the formerly very dry patch of my garden is evidently in view because—

"Is that *cabbage*?" Gita exclaims in shock.

"Yes!" I exclaim right back. "It's *cabbage!* Cabbage!" I let out a loud hooray.

"Okay, okay, we see it." Gita laughs. "We see the cabbage."

"Reyna, *choodu!* Look!" I say. "Baby cabbages!"

Reyna looks perplexed at my joy. "Very cool, Ammamma . . ."

Personally, I don't think either of them gets the hype at all, so I try again. "These haven't grown here since I was around your age, Gita. My ammamma used to make cabbage *koora* all the time. And to think Reyna's never even seen one!"

"What? I see them all the time," Reyna protests. "Amma made cabbage *koora* last week!"

"Yes, *kanna*," I say, "but that's that hydroponic shit you people grow over there. The real stuff is grown in the *dirt*. Real soil. Real food."

"Okay, Amma, let's not get into this again," Gita says, clearly miffed. "Hydroponics have fed a *lot* of people over the last fifty years. But I'm very happy for you about your cabbages. You can Iris us once they ripen, and we can make cabbage *koora* together. Reyna and I with our 'hydroponic shit' and you with your 'of-the-dirt' stuff."

We dream for a while together about cabbage *koora*, until Gita declares that it's bedtime for them over on Ojibwe Land.

I disconnect from Iris and allow the shimmering afternoon to envelop me. I slip my shoes off and dig my feet into moist soil. I feel my pulse.

tha ki ta tha ki ta—gin na
tha ki ta tha ki ta—gin na

My back hurts more often these days, and the asthma's been back for nearly twenty years (one can't blame my lungs—they put up a heroic fight against nearly half a century of summer wildfire smoke). I've had my share of cancer scares, too, like the rest of us.

tha ki ta tha ki ta—gin na

I think of the two generations before me, who saw the world change so much in their own lifetimes: my ammamma, watching India gain independence from the British Raj, and my amma, moving to a completely different continent and building a new life from scratch.

I think of the two generations after me: Gita, who didn't see stars for the first three decades of her life until regulations helped clear the smog. Reyna, who's never seen the snow but can do thirty-one *chakkar* and accompanies her mom to volunteer for ceremonial burn support.

tha ki ta tha ki ta—gin na

I think of the descendants who will follow, from whom I borrow this earth.

And in the cabbage patch, loam between my toes . . .

> *tha ki ta tha ki ta—gin na—dha*
> *—gin na—dha*
> *—gin na—dha*
> . . . I dance.

A Seder in Siberia

Louis Evans

The cupboards locked, the kitchen swept clean with a broom of pine twigs, the children each dressed in their one good outfit—a sleight of hand transforming a band of free-range ragamuffins into a sort of pocket-size town council—the sun creeping down, down, down toward the boreal horizon, and at last none of us could deny it: Jonathan wasn't coming.

So now all that remained was to tell Mom.

I tried first, because I'm weak.

"Don't you think it's time to go get Dad?"

"Miriam, your father's tired," she told me. Which is one way to say "dying of cancer," I suppose. She was setting the table for the third time. "Besides, your brother will be here any minute. *Then* we'll get Dad. Don't be impatient."

I bit my lip to keep from shouting. We had sworn a sacred sibling oath not to yell at her, but she did not make it easy.

David's turn.

"Maybe we should get started anyway, and Jonathan can *join*—"

"Just *wait*. I told your sister—"

"Do you even know *when*—"

"He'll *be* here—"

"Have you even spoken to him?"

"I sent a vid—he's very busy."

Despite my resolution, that pushed me back over the edge. I was bitterly grateful that my wife was stuck with her herds tonight; she hates to see me angry.

"You don't even know Jonathan's coming at all!"

"Miriam, I *said* I sent—"

"You don't even know if he *got* it, the loons—"

And then Leo spoke.

He didn't have to shout; he never does. It's funny how the baby of the family became the one we all listen to.

"Mom," said Leo. "Jonathan's not coming."

Silence filled the house, and darkness, too, with only a sliver of sun left and the candles not yet lit.

The seder was my father's domain. Everything about it was his, year after year. The seder plate was his seder plate. The moldy Haggadot, spiral-bound with ancient fossil plastic, were his. Even the recipes, suitably modified for our new agriculture (hazelnut matzah and algae karpas) came from his family. And, of course, he was the leader of the service, reading the familiar story word for word, year after year.

This was not the first seder of his illness.

Last year, when my shrunken and sallow father had taken his shuffling place at the head of our seder table, a remarkable transformation overtook him. It was as if the winds of other times and other places filled him like an airship, and suddenly he was not a suffering, shriveled, cancer-crossed dad; he was my father from childhood, from out of every childhood, from when the world was new.

For the fourth cup of wine, for the fourth promise of G-d, he read, just like every year of my life, "I will take you to be MY people," and deep in my bones I felt the truth of it, that I was of G-d's people and *of my father's people.*

That was the man my father was. Had been.

This was not the first seder of his illness. But it was the first seder of his death.

Dad entered the dining room, with Mom holding his elbow. He made it to his chair. He sat down.

Nothing happened.

We all sat there for a minute, in unfamiliar silence, even the children waiting for what would happen next. Dad blinked at the Haggadah Mom carefully placed in front of him. He tried to lift the first page.

It was too much for him; he let it fall.

I found myself, of course, looking to Leo at the foot of the table, and I knew David across from me was looking to him also, and my kids began to squirm, and Leo's face as he stared at Dad showed no legible emotion at all—

"I guess I'll read," said Mom.

✻

What is Passover?

David's the schoolteacher. He's good at explanations. Me, I don't explain anything. I just gene-tweak mammoths.

Working as an eco-pheno-geno-biofeedback climate engineer, you get in the habit of seeing things as very complicated. Is this stand of old-growth taiga spruce a valuable carbon sink? Or is it a "bad voxel" with a dangerously low albedo compared to adjacent snowy grasslands, primed to absorb too much sunlight and turn it into heat? Or is it a useful landmark for navigating a mammoth herd? Or is that bad because we want to lure the herd onto a different track to reduce the risk of interherd conflict? Or . . .

I write a lot of reports.

Passover is a holiday that celebrates the liberation of the Jews from Egypt *and/or* Passover is a collection of songs and stories and quizzes and weird little games, like a mixed-up child's toy chest of traditions *and/or* Passover is when twenty million of the world's most anxious people get to explore a fun, seasonal set of dietary restrictions in addition to the year-round ones *and/or* Passover is the candles, and the wine, and the prayers, and the songs, *and/or* Passover is a story of a marvelous escape by refugees trapped between an army and an ocean . . .

I write a lot of reports, and then I go in and change the mammoths. Back in the Pleistocene, extremely long biofeedback loops took care of that automatically, but these days we are on a tighter timetable. So I made the mammoths snow white; that was me. The genetic sequence from polar bears is very well characterized, and it takes transcription easily. A white mammoth absorbs less sunlight; the glittering fur reflects more heat back into space. Every good voxel counts.

What is Passover?

Basically, you get all your family in one room, deny everybody food until you've made it through a two-hour interactive lecture, while constantly drinking more and more wine, and then act surprised when a fight breaks out.

"Mom, don't you think . . ." said David. But she hadn't listened to him for forty-two years; why would she start now?

"Now in the presence of loved ones and friends, before us the emblems of festive rejoicing . . ."

She was off. What could we do? We read along, all of us chorusing in unison, siblings, spouses, kids, even Dad managing to mumble.

"Remember the day on which you went forth from Egypt, from the house of bondage."

And what do you know, she was good.

It was a little cynical, perhaps, to judge my own mother's reading of the seder strictly on its theatrical merits, but surely we Jews have earned our cynicism. And she was good. Deep voice, solid rhythm. Kept good time in the group readings and didn't interrupt the kids when they stumbled over the longer, more ornate words and transliterations. I didn't have to hate this.

So long as I kept my eyes off Dad.

Seder in English literally translates as "order." Nevertheless, our family never reads the Haggadah in the official order. Instead, the whole thing is held together by a complicated web of bookmarks and marginal notes. It's not the original system, but it works.

That's why, not twenty minutes into the seder, between the first and second cups of wine, we got to Elijah.

There's a superstition about Elijah. You leave an extra cup of wine out for him, and then you send the little kids to open the door for Elijah. Then one of the adults sneaks the glass of wine, or secretly rocks the table, and "Look, kids, it's Elijah, he's drinking it!"

In the book of Kings, Elijah smites hundreds with fire from heaven. In the Haggadah, he plays a silly little haunted-house drinking game with kids. Being a grown-up is like that, I think.

"May the All-Merciful send us Elijah the Prophet to comfort us with tidings of deliverance," said Mom. "Now let us open the door for Elijah."

David and my kids knew their parts, and they ran, all in a giggling mob, to the front door to fling it open—

And they *screamed*.

⁂

The man at the door did look like Elijah. He was tall, and gaunt, and bearded. He was bundled for the taiga, not the deserts of the Holy Land, but his clothes were stark and worn. One arm was tied up in an impromptu sling.

I must have run for the door when the kids screamed; we all must have. I don't remember; I never remember running to my kids. I just remember staring, and staring, and *staring* at the man standing in the doorway.

It had been years. There was no reason that the kids should recognize their uncle Jonathan.

⁂

Mom bustled Jonathan in the door, and she bustled the door shut. She bustled him out of his traveling clothes, and she worried over his injured arm so much that she almost fainted. She ran back and forth with ever-increasing energy and declining effectiveness until Leo stopped her.

He got her back into her chair at the head of the table, got Jonathan seated at the foot beside him. Dad had not stood up to greet Jonathan; I did not know if he understood that Jonathan had been gone and now he was back. I didn't know.

David asked Jonathan about his arm. "Grolar bear attack," he replied.

It wasn't surprising. We've been driving up the population of grolars for years now. Larger apex predators produce upward cull pressure on herbivore size, which increases winter survivability and population throughput, ultimately allocating more biomass to the mammoths overall. But push it up too hard and you kick off a predation double bust, which throws your whole cycle out of whack, and so on.

Systems are complicated.

The kids were probably desperate to ask Jonathan about the grolars, but they were still scared of him, and he didn't seem inclined to talk much. So I didn't ask any follow-up questions, and neither did David.

"Mom," said Leo, "keep reading."

Jonathan started in his seat, turning to Leo. "Dad reads," he said.

Leo did not turn to face him. They had been so close, before, the baby of the family and the eldest; Leo had idolized Jonathan. Jonathan was the sort of man Leo had always wanted to be, since long before the rest of us even knew he would grow into one. But then Jonathan vanished. No surprise Leo took it hard.

"This year Mom reads," he said.

Jonathan looked at Leo. Looked at Mom. Looked at Dad. Looked away.

In a dining room crowded for seder, it's hard to find somewhere to look that's not another watching face, but he managed.

Mom was still staring at her prodigal son, drinking in his face, but Leo caught her eye and gave her a firm nod, and she started reading again.

Passover is a child-friendly holiday. Not really the story of the Exodus itself, which has an unavoidable infusion of the Bronze Age macabre (drowned babies, Moses beating and killing an overseer, blood on the doorpost, spontaneous death plague), but certainly the seder is. The songs have an easy nursery rhyme simplicity. The ritual food appears in handy sandwich format. The children have dedicated readings; "Ma Nishtanah"—"Why is this night different from all other nights?"—is traditionally sung by the youngest child present.

But the Four Children is not, I think, exactly child friendly.

It's an odd little bit of text, a piece of Talmudic psychological gristle undigested by medieval pageantry or modern bowdlerization. It notices that the Torah commands us to teach our children the story of Passover four distinct times. Now, a mammoth geneticist would see that reduplication as merely a healthy copy-error redundancy in an inherited text, but the rabbis of the Talmud thought differently. They thought that every word was a perfect, unique gift from G-d.

So they said that four commandments meant four different ways to teach; four different archetypal children. The wise child, the wicked child, the simple child, and the one who does not even know how to ask. Each of them receives a different instruction.

The passage is child unfriendly, not through sex or violence, but rather through its crushing essentialism. These days we tell our children, "You can be anything you want to be." These days we tell them, "You live in a special time, an important time, when there is so much work of *tikkun olam*, of repairing Earth. So much work, so many jobs—from rewilding the rainforest to herding mammoths!—and one of those jobs out there is just for you. Just as special and unique as you are."

But our sages teach us: There are four children. Kiss-ass, shit-head, stupid, and double stupid.

In my family there were four of us too.

Don't imagine that we missed that part.

※

In the end, it was simple bad luck.

Most of the readings in our Haggadah are delivered solo by the leader, or together by the entire table. But the Four Children is tagged with that most perilous note, "A Participant." Which means we go around the table, clockwise.

I had the wise child. That gave Leo the wicked.

"The wicked person says, 'What is this observance to *you?*' Because they say 'to *you*' and not 'to *us*,' they reject the unity of G-d and the community of Judaism. To them we respond sharply"—suddenly Leo was looking at Jonathan, staring at him, teeth flashing as he bit out words—"it is because of what G-d did for *me* when *I* went forth from Egypt, for by abandoning us, *you* would not have known redemption."

Time for the chorus, and David and I leapt in. "The wicked one withdraws themselves from anything beyond themselves." Mom was reading along, and the kids were doing their best, and even Dad was gamely mumbling, but Jonathan didn't say anything. Neither did Leo.

We trailed off, a comet tail of phonetic rubble. Jonathan's turn now, but he still wasn't saying anything. His Haggadah lay open on the table, still open to the page of the wicked child.

"Jonathan," I said in the gentlest voice I could manage. "It's your turn."

My older brother has never listened to me.

"I don't deserve this," Jonathan said to Leo.

All across Leo's face I could see pain congealing into anger.

"Of course you do," Leo said. "You left. One day, you just got it into your head to leave us."

"No," said Jonathan. "Dad told me to go."

Jonathan left us when he was nineteen. There was no warning.

He'd been fighting with Dad more. I think. It was hard to tell. Jonathan and Dad both had a strange, oblique way of arguing. Nothing like me or David or Mom. Just a coldness that settled between words, between actions, that froze the ground and then kept it frozen. And then one day he was gone.

Leo was fourteen; he'd come out a year and a half earlier. (He's the only Jew I know who's had both a bat and a bar mitzvah. Good timing.) When Jonathan left, Leo felt abandoned by his brother. He was devastated.

But the rest of us were hurting too.

It's a big world out there, and we lived at the very farthest edge of it. I understood that. I could imagine how Jonathan might want to see something different from tundra, tundra, tundra, mammoth. I could imagine how Jonathan might want to escape from the cold in our house and the cold in our family. I could imagine lots of things.

I had to imagine because he never videoed, never even DMed.

There's internet service at the house, at least when the loons—network-relay balloons, high up in the stratosphere—form a tight enough chain. These days that's most days, since they keep putting them up in the stratosphere. Shiny Mylar, *amazing* albedo. Very good voxels. Back when Jonathan left, two decades ago, the service was less regular. But he could have at least DMed.

He never did.

Well, he never DMed *me*.

"What?" said Leo.

"Dad told me to go."

"Just because he threw you out of the house didn't mean you had to leave the continent!"

"No. It wasn't like that. He sent me back."

"He *what*?"

Mom broke in. "You two can catch up later. The simple child—"

Leo stopped her with an outstretched arm.

"Dad *sent* you? Why? *Where*?"

Jonathan shuffled uncomfortably in his seat. He was a big man, even if thinned out from his taiga journey home, but he seemed all at once to collapse in on himself.

"I dunno. Ask him."

Leo's eyes narrowed. He turned to look at Dad.

Dad stared blankly back at all of us. He blinked. He licked his lips. I do not know if, at that moment, he could have counted his own children.

"Well?" said Leo. "Where did you send him?"

Dad blinked again.

"The simple child asks, 'What is this?' To them—"

"Where did you send Jonathan, Dad?"

". . . we say, 'With a mighty arm'—"

"Where did you send Jonathan?" Leo's voice was louder than I'd heard it in years.

"'. . . G-d freed us'—"

"Where did Jonathan go?" Leo was shouting now, hands flat on the table.

"'. . . from the house of bondage.'"

"Where, Dad!"

"Texas," said Mom. "He wanted us to go home."

"Dad's not from Texas," said David.

"Home is *here*," I said at the same time.

It's hard to say which one of us Mom looked at with greater contempt. But she loved Leo, and she spoke to him.

"We never told you," she said. "We didn't want you to know."

"Dad's not from Texas," said David. "We're not from Texas. If we were from Texas—"

"You didn't move here," I said. "You were sent."

✳

Jewish history is a litany of expulsions. First exile, second exile. The Roman Diaspora. The Spanish Inquisition. The Khmelnytsky Uprising. The pogroms. The Holocaust. These episodes enter gentile history as genocides, as exterminations, and this is not inaccurate. But the Jews of a later era are descended from survivors, and survivors *fled*. They knew when to flee and how fast to travel.

The story of the Exodus is perhaps not a surprise.

✳

"You could have told us," said David. "There's no shame in it. Half of my class's parents are from Texas. They made new lives, they raised families, they *talk* about it—"

"Yes," said Leo. "*They* talk about it." He was still staring at Dad. Dad blinked aimlessly, then blinked again with sudden recognition and said, quite clearly and distinctly, "Jonathan."

Silence fell over the seder table.

"Jonathan," he said again. But he was not looking at his oldest son; he was looking at his youngest.

"Yes, Dad," said Leo quietly.

"Jonathan, you're back."

"Yes, Dad," said Leo, and beside him Jonathan mouthed the same words.

"Jonathan, did they forgive me? Can I go home?"

Leo clenched his jaw, his fists. He turned to his older brother.

"No, Dad," said Jonathan. "You can't."

❈

What happened in Texas was complicated. Drought in the Rio Grande. Crop failures across the Great Plains, from Nuevo León to Iowa. Mass migration along several distinct axes. Dismemberment of the petrochemical industry. Rocket riots over Project Sunshade. Paramilitary violence and military violence.

System failures are as complicated as systems themselves.

But not everyone who left Texas was a refugee.

❈

"They took me to a museum," Jonathan said. "I marched in and applied for family repatriation, and they looked my name up on a list and said, 'You'd better come with us.' And I thought—"

I do not think I had ever seen my brother cry before. Nobody needed to ask him what he thought.

"But I went and they *showed* me, Dad. The Hall of Exiles. They have a museum and *you're in it*. They have the drone cams and the SWAT group chats and the interoffice wiki. Dozens of people *died* in that holding cell—"

"Hot summer," said Dad. He sounded ancient. He sounded like a boy.

"You had water and you *didn't give it to them*."

"Such a hot summer," said Dad. "They just kept coming."

"A new king arose over Egypt," I said, "and he said, 'Look, the Israelite people are too numerous for us. Let us then deal shrewdly with them.'"

"Hottest summer of my life," said Dad. "Nothing like here."

"Then *why did you send me back?*"

Dad stared for a long time. His jaw went slack.

"I want to go home."

*

We couldn't get anything out of Dad after that. He went back inside, to where that metastatic shadow-self was eating him.

*

The next day, out on the range with my wife, checking in on the pregnant mammoths and tagging the youngest calves, telling her the story, I could not believe it didn't end right then. But the truth is, we kept going. None of us were ready for the seder to end.

We drank all four cups of wine. We counted out the plagues. We ate algae karpas and horseradish from the backyard. The kids hid the hazelnut afikomen. Leo hugged Jonathan. Jonathan hugged Mom. The mammoth brisket was delicious. We sang "Dayenu," because even a single miracle would have been enough.

Out on the range with Thea, I thought about my parents' lies. About my father's crimes. About fleeing, and being sent.

When a loon is near, I could look up my father's trial. I could dig up his conviction in an old database. I don't need to, though. The sentences were all the same. *Climate remediation for the remainder of natural life.* Forty years in the desert.

Those sentenced ended up all over. The olam is wide, and there's more than enough tikkun to go around. "It is not your duty to finish the work, but neither are you at liberty to neglect it."

The world is very complicated, and sometimes when I try too

hard to understand it all, I get confused. Which is why I'm grateful for my wife.

She gets up in the morning. She puts her feet on the permafrost. She tends to the mammoths.

To me, those animals are 5.8 billion genetic base pairs locked in a chaos cascade with maybe half a trillion other ecological variables, bending the curve of an ecosystem away from catastrophe. That's what I write in my reports.

Thea doesn't think about them that way. She puts her hands on a snowy, furry flank; a trunk wraps around her shoulders. That's enough.

So I told her the story, all of it, and I waited at the end for her insight. And because she's wiser than I am, she waited instead for me. And I realized: I know how the story ends. The same way it always does: *l'shana haba'ah b'yerushalayim.*

Next year, in a more just world. Next year, in the city of peace.

The Imperfect Blue Marble

Rae Mariz

Lærke's first word was *wing*.

She lay cradled between the moss and her mama, watching the branches cut the sky in precise patterns. Her poor ma Suzume had fallen asleep after chasing the child around the farm, trying to keep Lærke's tongue out of the beehive. The city's colorful turbine balloons hovered high in the atmosphere, silently harvesting wind—and look there, the giggle of a single cumulonimbus in an otherwise blue sky.

Little Lærke's developing mind observed the canopy overhead, babbling her wordless song above the comforting thunder of her mother's snores. Then the word took shape on her lips and flew. *Wing*. Out into the world.

Auntie Cade looked up from the sacred text her needle had been working, the folds of fabric bunched in her lap. She'd been humming the ballad as she stitched those lessons of the living land, quietly harmonizing with the baby's joyful yoller, but fell silent when she heard the word. The child's first!

She followed Lærke's gaze up to the sky, expecting to identify which dot in the kaleidoscope of community kites had caught the child's attention, then eased herself down beside the babe to see from her perspective. Which of those turbine balloons or spinning kites and whipping dragontails in the skies had teased the first word from the baby's lips?

Maybe that one? One of the neighbor's blimp turbine designs had dual blades that flashed like hummingbird wings—not the most efficient design, but since when had creativity been overly concerned with efficiency? It was certainly eye-catching.

Instead, as Auntie Cade nestled back close to the baby, cheek to cheek, Lærke showed her auntie a butterfly wing swirling dust motes ignited by the sunlight.

"That's right, *wing*," Auntie Cade affirmed and pulled the Field Guide blanket up over the three of them. They snuggled in under the weight of wisdoms passed from auntie to auntie— woven, crafted, compiled—while Lærke and her auntie watched the butterfly dance in the golden pollen.

We always say a child's first word is a gift.

And look at that.

. . .

You're . . . hm. You're not watching the butterfly. Look . . .

The blue of the butterfly wing is not a pigment; the color is formed by a delicate structure that refracts light itself, much like the blue of the sky. No real surprise that the beauty of chaos has been represented in the motion of—

You seem distracted. What are you looking for? Me? You're wondering who this person is, telling you to look here and there. You want to know who's telling the story? Fine.

I am a storyteller. The storyteller. This story's teller.

There's no use scanning the edges of the scene trying to find me. I'm not perched on a boulder beside these three as they're experiencing this intimate, poignant moment on this lovely day. You think I'm up in a tree looking down on the scene? With these knees? Please.

I'm omniscient, but I'm not a creeper.

You can most often find me in the Tangle, the place in the city where paths converge. I don't have to be present at every moment to know what's going on. People tell me things. I have a trust-worthy face.

Step closer. Let me get a good look at you. Knowing who we're telling the story to is part of the craft: "The storyteller assesses their audience." Watches the people as they mingle in the Tangle. Notes the dress of the passerby, their manner. A storyteller wouldn't tell the same story to the lonely child seeking solace in the storyteller's lap as they would to the bawdy crowd on their way to a fertility show.

Or at least, *I* wouldn't tell it in the same *way*.

Any decent storyteller has this skill. It's the same observations about character that we weave into our tales. *Is the listener in a rush? Are they looking for escape? Do they need a single golden spider-web thread to sew together something frayed inside?*

Some storytellers tailor their tales to what their listeners want. My training taught me to look for the story the listener didn't know they needed.

And you. A *reader* from the tail end of the blip era, what story do you need from me? Am I even able to tell you a story you will understand? You're most likely steeped in the narrative techniques of the settler literatures of the time. Tricky . . . but difficult things are not impossible, and I wouldn't be a storyteller if I didn't like a challenge. Besides, you're in luck. Though the story trends popular in the twenty-first century have long gone out of style, I just so happen to enjoy experimenting with this outdated form. I'm afraid that most current storytellers have found that the simplistic structures you're familiar with often fail to capture our children's imaginations, so they've largely been left for archival scholars to catalog as a hobby. I have a friend who does this. Winslowe. He finds it relaxing. *Hero goes on a journey* or *A stranger comes to town*. His husband, Jibril, finds it tedious, but I admire people who are passionate about their passions! Whatever makes him happy, we agree.

Let me tell you about their son, Ben.

Aunties aren't supposed to have favorites, and they don't. Hierarchical thinking isn't actually natural to human cognition, and there isn't any scarcity of resources to compete over. Especially in regard to a person's capacity for love.

If you ask Auntie Cade though, and I have (storytellers ask the *most* impertinent questions, get used to it), she was uniquely grateful for Ben. We all were, but part of that was due to Auntie Cade's . . . interpretations . . . as she decoded the intricacies of his language. It turned out to not be a private language, like maybe his parents and peers, cousins, siblings, storytellers, neighbors, and neithers assumed. Ben was in communication with all the unheard and mostly unseen, outside the spectrum of general human understanding.

I don't want to make this telling of a slight, autistic Black boy to sound unnecessarily mystical or mythical. He's a person. But sometimes one's love for a person embellishes their qualities—they swell with our regard, inflating like a generator blimp before we hoist them high. Once a storyteller gets their hands on a person, they make the character appear larger than life. Is this the mark of fine craftsmanship or a rookie mistake? (You can tell me, it won't hurt my feelings.) Why shouldn't the loving renderings of an artist's brush caress a child, stroke his cheek, and tickle his armpits?

Ben would hate it, so that's one reason not to. And the only reason we need.

Of all the children she'd taught and inspired, nurtured and guided and delighted in, Auntie Cade recognized that she'd learned the most from Ben. She told us that Ben showed her things; he'd shown them to all of us, but sometimes it required an auntie's attention to understand a child.

Our culture puts a lot of weight on a baby's first word. (See above.) Not so much *what* the baby says, mostly *that* the baby says. That they've arrived at a phase of language acquisition which marks their inclusion in the community conversation.

Feral cats don't meow. Or so the story goes.

We talk about *everything*. People do. The ASL sign for a hearing person simulates words tumbling from the mouth. We're always talking. Especially the people I know. It varies from neighborhood to neighborhood, culture to culture. But for the most part, we've evolved, especially since your time—those blip generations when decisions were made by might, hierarchical decree, or just not made at all—we've learned how to talk things out.

When there is a problem, we gather. And talk. Not to be

heard, but to discuss. We approach the discussion acknowledging that there is a problem, and that the solution is not yet known, because if any one person knew how to solve that problem, it wouldn't be an issue, now, would it? If it were a problem easily solved, we would've made quick work of ensuring it *wasn't* a problem. We would instead be off braiding bread or rinsing the vegetable inks from the pages of a library book and searching the catalog for a new one to print—living our lives. No, if we're there in that room, in that clearing, filling that field, meeting in a sports arena—then we have a problem so tricky that it needs everyone's input. Children as young as six years old have contributed to civic matters. Do voices get raised? Sure. Do men burst into tears? Quite often. Do passions drown out reasoned accounts? Eh, not as often as you fear. Our children learn to listen at a young age and become adept in the skill as adults.

I see it straining your imagination, Stranger Comes to Town, that the opinions of each individual in a mob could be worthy of respect. Do not feel bad about your disability. We see it as a failure of education . . . one of the many things lost in the blip generations, along with the 83 percent loss of biodiversity in the sixth mass extinction event you are currently living through.

But we were talking about Ben. How could a culture of loud-mouths appreciate a quiet kid? Who grew to be a silent adult?

Because, unlike the "domesticated" cat, most of the wild creatures we share a planet with didn't go out of their way to try and learn our language. To vocalize their need, to pitch their voices like a baby's cry, to trigger a physiological response that requires immediate attention from people who hear it. Feral cats are silent because they don't want to attract attention to themselves or communicate with people. They want to be left the hell alone.

Animals have rich languages of scents and gestures and vo-calization patterns. Able to communicate between themselves and with one another, and very few of *us* have gone out of our way to understand the linguistic complexities of our fellows. Not with the same determination of the cats, at least. "But could those things really be considered *language?*" I hear one of you say. Your white sciences change the definitions and shift the goalposts every time a community of creatures approximates those arbitrary markers for intelligence, sentience, life. Every time. To ensure that only human people stand in the circle—and terrifyingly often, it's only the people with similar qualities of those enforcing the definitions who are allowed in. Personally, I tend to wonder if that culture built on exclusion, exhausting itself to enforce artificial borders (or otherwise centering a single person's narrative thread, and consequently relegating the rest to less-important supporting characters and background greenery) may have led to the worldview that brought your generation so close to ending the ever-generating world.

So yes, I say language.

Listen to birdsong as you walk through a place with birds. I was going to say "the woods," but that might be difficult for you to find, presently. Things were dire at the tail end of the blip era. As I understand it, you were so very successful in excluding everything unlike your kind . . . Anyway, walk among birds. Listen to their trilling call-and-response. You can be sure that they are talking, and I guarantee they are talking *about you*. You are big news in the woods. They are not quite sure what to make of you. Are you a predator? What have you done to assure the birds that you are not a threat? It's easy enough to show them. Their birdsong is asking. They are waiting for a reply.

Ben's first "word" was a reply. Our culture has a parallel language system of gestures; yours might too. A thumbs-up, a corny salute. A peace sign, a fuck you. Our neighborhood has a gesture of gratitude—two fingers pressed to one's own lips. Thank you. And one to express a wordless need—hands cupped into an empty bowl. You would probably try to find the words for this feeling . . . general malaise, vague disappointment, unfulfilled desire, a soft sense of regret. You know the feeling. It's just a nameless funk. Instead of trying to locate the feeling, to understand it—or jerkily act out in desperation to feel anything else—our people tend to just signal the inner turmoil we're experiencing by cupping our hands into an empty bowl. Close to the body if we want to be left alone with the feeling, extended out from the body if we need someone to pull us out of it. It's useful. Easy to communicate. Both for oneself and to others. The prevalence of tragic instances of ill-advised bang cutting in our society has diminished, at least.

When Ben was maybe three—long past the age most expect to welcome their children through the rites of their first word—Auntie Cade was walking alongside Ben during their daily route through the Tangle. She would follow where he led, always close enough should he need her, but never insisting on holding his hand in the crowded public space. He didn't like for his hand to be held, and it's easy enough to allow small children their autonomy generally, Ben in particular. His morning routine was sacred to him, and he was never at risk of running off.

On this day, Auntie Cade witnessed Ben making his quiet wander to his favorite places. He watched the glassblower turn sand into exquisite shapes—mesmerized by the lava blobs birthed in fire and brought to life with breath. The glassblower was a small man with thinning hair and a quiet voice. He did his work, seemingly indifferent to Ben's constant presence—a feat, since people are otherwise hyperaware of a three-year-old in the vicinity of molten stoves and display shelves of delicate glassworks. But the glassblower had come to an agreement with Ben, an arrangement. Each day, the glassmaker dropped a single glass marble into a large, wide bowl just as Ben was ready to leave, in gratitude for the child's attention and as thanks for him not touching all his stuff or breaking anything.

Ben listened to the smooth, nearly frictionless vibrations as the marble rolled in a path up the sides of the bowl and around. Ben's eyes followed the lazy arcs and parabolas, and when it tinkled to a stop in the center, Ben reached in with his small fingers and picked it up. He examined the color and the finish of the marble, weighed it in his hand, and, satisfied after his appraisal, placed the marble he'd carried around all the previous day onto the rim of the bowl and let it circle to rest at the center. Then he left the workshop with the new marble nestled in his palm.

I asked the glassblower about this ritual and about the day it changed. I had to tease the story out of him, slowly, like the expanding bubble of glass. He told me it started as a simple token, the kind he often gave children in gratitude for not touching any of the fragile wares. The first one was rather large—Ben was still small, and there were no assurances that he wouldn't put it in his mouth. (Auntie Cade assures me that he never did, which she found odd, since he put everything else in his mouth at that time—except for a variety of foods she hoped he would like.) Ben carried the fistful of smooth glass cupped in his chubby hand the whole day, and when the glassmaker presented him with a new one the next day, baby Ben deposited the old one and clutched the new. That was what intrigued the glassmaker. He'd assumed Ben would collect them like other children often did. He'd meant for the baby to have both. All of them.

We don't like to use words like exchange or trade. They're so rooted in blip characterizations of transactional relationships that we just . . . find more accurate words. But Ben started this ritual, and each morning, the child plucked the new gift from the bowl, examined it, then returned the one from yesterday before accepting the new one. Until one day when Ben picked up the day's marble and, for whatever reason, preferred to keep hold of the one he had, and let the new one slide back into the bowl.

The glassmaker was startled, curious, and after the boy left, he picked up the marble and examined it. It was of the same quality as all the other marbles. What inspired the child's preference for the previous? "There were no imperfections," the glassblower told me while clipping a molten blob of glass. It curled in on itself like a living larva. "But there was some quality that displeased him, or at least persuaded Ben to keep holding on to the one in his hand." Here I had to wait some time for the glassblower to roll his rod and use gravity to temper and shape the glob that would become a kind of vase. "That's when it started. It went from a game to a challenge to . . ." He stared thoughtfully at the fires. "An inspiration. I am so grateful to Ben. His careful regard has inspired the development of my craft to a degree that no one else would probably notice, but I know that *he* notices. Propelled by the urge to please him, my craft has been elevated to art and then to an act of devotion. I'm still not sure what the boy is looking for when he makes his assessments. It's not perfection. Perfection is easy compared to this. I just want to make something that makes him happy. Something he wants to carry around with him each day, every day."

I asked the glassblower if he'd ever felt offended. Refusing a gift can be a sensitive matter. The glassblower was startled. "It never occurred to me to be offended. You know Ben. The social rules of the gift don't apply. It's just him and me and the day's marble."

I later learned that on the day I'm taking my sweet time in telling you about, the moment that Ben joined the extended family of the living world, Ben had been holding on to the same marble for two ten-days. That marble was blue, with cloudy swirls of white and flecks of green-brown. The glassblower had presented him with twenty examples of his refined craft—some vibrantly colored and particularly large or remarkably small, since the glassblower was getting kind of desperate to create something that would win the boy's favor—and none of them satisfied Ben's internal matrices of color, feel, and weight that made a gift a pleasure to hold.

"I still have no idea what it was about that one that appealed to the kid." He let his sigh shape glass. "It was even slightly misshapen, with a bit of a bulge around the equator. Not at all my best work."

But this was the one Ben didn't want to let go of. Come, let's go catch up with him. You'll soon realize why I spent a seemingly disproportionate amount of time imbuing so much meaning into a smooth chunk of glass a three-year-old carried clutched in his grasp. There he is. He's moved on from the glassblower's workshop to watch the rivermen unload their shares on the Main Stream docks, with Auntie Cade shadowing alongside him.

The crew rolled barrels onto shore, tilted them upright in a row. Ben watched them pop the tops off the barrels and plunge their hands elbows-deep into the watery contents. They wrestled strands of kelp from inside and strung them, glistening, up on a line, so the sunshine glinted off the slick surfaces, highlighting the variety of each. The exquisite variations in colors and textures and shapes.

Red sea kelp, which eases digestion processes in ruminants, decreases the methane content of cow farts—and can also fry up crisp and salty like bacon. Tasty. Exotic sugar kelp harvested from Nordic shores, alongside eelgrass gleaned from local seagrass meadows. Ben silently regarded the hanging kelp strands glittering like festive garlands, their home waters draining back into the barrels beneath, while people stopped to admire and inquire.

"Pretty big haul today," Jibril's voice boomed out, and he rested his big dad hand on Ben's back. Ben flinched away from the touch. "Oh, sorry, Benevolence," Jibril apologized and glanced at Auntie Cade.

She admonished him with a twitch of the corner of her mouth and nodded encouragement.

Jibril knelt beside his son and lowered his voice. "I thought I'd find you by the boats. You like the boats?"

Ben didn't answer or meet his eyes. He poked at one of the slimy air bladders bobbing on the surface in the sea barrel.

Jibril joined him in pinching and stroking the glistening seaweed and started to make conversation with the rivermen.

"These specimens are a delight," Jibril said. "I don't think I've seen sugar kelp available for some time. Rough seas?"

"No more than usual." The riverman shrugged as she ladled more seawater on the strung-up strands to keep them glistening and hydrated. "Hydrofoil yacht pirates are always trying to take more than their share, but these beauties came through from the kelp farms of Sør-Trøndelag."

"They've come so far!" Jibril exclaimed, "Ben, this seawater is from the far seas. Incredible."

Ben continued to poke the air bladders, obviously sharing his dad's fascination with the seaweed, though maybe not for the same reasons.

Everyone called Winslowe "Ben's dad" and Jibril "Ben's big dad" (Ben, of course, didn't refer to them at all). Jibril was, yes, a hulk of a man, but it was his outgoing personality that gave him his "big dad" stature. He and his mama, Kerime, kept a community tavern attached to the Archives, where he and Winslowe and Ben had a small living space above the library. "You're off-loading?" Jibril made note of the number of barrels.

"Most of it. We talked to Lis, who said the salvage crew approved a rebuild of the generator serving East Bear cluster, so when needs are met here, we're taking the river algae to the technicians. They can use their mysterious chemistries to extract materials for self-repairing sail production. You want anything today?"

"No need, no need. Only when I saw you had so much, it inspired me. I have an idea for a new recipe I wouldn't mind serving up at the tavern today . . ."

Ben wandered off to his next stop at the witchcrafters while his big dad invited the rivermen over for a hearty meal, whether or not they had sugar kelp to spare. Auntie Cade followed the boy, sure he was eager to play with the puppies Auntie Owen had been bringing to the circle while they all talked story and swapped dyeing methods and stitch techniques. But Auntie Cade soon realized that she'd lost sight of the boy. He had veered off from his usual route, and she searched the crowd at knee height, looking for him, fighting back a strange shame—an auntie never loses sight of their child. (Though Auntie Cade is quite extreme in her sense of responsibilities. She doesn't permit herself to make mistakes, when everyone else knows that aunties are only human.)

Then she saw him. Tottering over to a man she didn't recognize. Not a neighbor, perhaps a neither. That's what we call people who we don't yet have a named relationship with. You call them strangers, which . . . rude. But the man was sitting crouched off to the side with his head down and his cupped hands held out. Ben had noticed him, probably glimpsed between the legs of passersby, and had left his prescribed route to answer him.

Ben slipped his tiny hand into the man's empty cupped ones.

The man looked up, startled, and opened his hands to find that Ben had placed the glassmaker's marble there. The colorful work of magic. The cold miniature world.

Tears streamed down Auntie Cade's cheeks when she saw Ben take the man's hand, urge him to his feet, and lead him over to the puppies. She knew how Ben felt about holding hands, that he endured his own discomfort to give comfort to another. She hurried the few steps back to Jibril to tearfully recount what had just happened. How Ben had recognized the man's need, and he had responded. This was unmistakably a word. Ben's first.

They embraced and laughed and wove through the crowds to the witchcrafters' circle. They found Ben silently introducing the man to the squirmy puppies, even then showing his abilities to be attuned to the nonverbal needs of creatures, human and otherwise.

I'm sure you know that's not the end. How could a first word ever be?

But you didn't need a story about an ending. I saw that right away, the first time we met there in the beginning. Saw how I would have to unspool my narrative thread into loose loops and coils to ensnare you. My needle sharp and glinting to repair the tears. It's a story, I hope, that will hold to bridge the short century between us. A tightrope that will help you find your way back here.

Even now, you're wondering how a storyteller from the future could be telling you all this. The, like . . . *mechanics* of the thing. See, storytellers are time travelers. Always have been. Or at least they could be, if they understood their true relationship with time. I'm not sure the blip storytellers were able to do this. The records of their stories would read differently if they could . . . though maybe the ones who understood the weavings of time didn't get the opportunity to leave records. (I'll have to talk with Winslowe about that one—archivists aren't wrong all the time.)

I'm not predicting the future. I'm just telling you what I've seen and been told. So the next time you find yourself holding on to an imperfect blue marble, you might have a few ideas about what to do with it.

By the Skin of Your Teeth

Gina McGuire

Disclaimer: This is a fictional work, and I do not advocate for readers to engage with sharks in the ways described without experience and/ or permission. This work was written to honor traditional practices of kahu manō, of shark guardianships in Hawai'i, as well as to identify marine- and Oceania-based climate solutions that are inclusive of and dependent on local and Indigenous islanders.

Offshore South Kona, Hawai'i Island
March 20, 2112
"Why are we out here again?" Kūkia's breath came out as small puffs of steam in the chill early morning air. The winters had gotten harsher, wetter and colder, just as the summers brought the bleaching, the water much too warm.

"Poachers," Māihi whispered grumpily. She was not a morning person, particularly on these crisp spring mornings. But it was she who had insisted they come out. Māihi had always liked the warm-muscle feeling in her legs that would come as they anchored her within to the deck in the rolling swell, and she focused on that now. They had been watching, waiting for over an hour.

"I don't think they're coming," Kūkia said sourly and shook his head, although he smiled behind his neck guard. He dangled his feet off the swim deck in small, lazy circles. One and Aka moved languidly beneath his toes with their gentle-giant way. The waters here were rich with the plankton they needed. He knew many of the manō by name, easily distinguished by their varying markings or scars, and would often spend the day free diving beside them, trying to immerse himself in their world of salt and humpback song. He began to sing softly, a song composed to honor Kanaloa, the *akua* of the sea world.

The pair gazed down at the slow movements of the large, graceful whale sharks and the gliding movements of the occasional ray below. The water was clear enough that they could make out the Alice-in-Wonderland outline of the reef below, some twenty or thirty feet down, and the undulating indentions in the sand that ran parallel to the shore behind them. Māihi's feet tapped an *'uwehe* into the deck: one foot lifted, weight held on the opposite hip, foot lowered, and knees pushed forward, heels raised. The four-step pop steadily followed the rhythm of the sea and boat's entwined heartbeat.

"We know they've been coming in the early morning," Māihi insisted quietly. If she closed her eyes, she could feel the rough sandpaper edge of sharkskin she sometimes saw at the market, the bins of fins secretly coveted as black-market medicine with the increasing levels of cancer among the islanders . . . and her anger would bubble through her, like a muscle spasm she couldn't control. So, she kept her eyes wide open.

"We have to stop them." She peered sideways at Kūkia, admiring his loose, long black hair. Her hands instinctively reached to the ends of her short hair and her *na'au* sank with the remembering. The four-step deck dance stopped.

Kūkia waited several moments before responding. "People are struggling."

It had been twenty years since the meat industry was shut down and US production had fully switched over to plant-based replacements; just ten years since Hawai'i had started the Seas Pathways program in partnership with other Oceania nations.

Kūkia, a few years older than Māihi, had been part of the project from the beginning as guardian of the manō's movement through *'Ōiwi* waters. He, himself, had never liked the idea of the plant-based proteins, of meat being made, and had watched with fear for his people as the rising protein prices had come along with the industry. He had watched as their waters had been increasingly fished by all those who couldn't afford the protein, returning to this ancestral icebox. And as the fish populations had declined, the hunger had turned toward the sharks. For meat, for leather, for spirit medicine. People weren't hungry, maybe, he reconciled within himself, but they were starved for *something*, the something that he and Māihi now guarded.

"Everything depends on them," Māihi said, her voice so low Kūkia almost couldn't hear her. "Everything." Since climate scientists had reported that large marine creatures, not just whales but also large sharks, large fish such as tuna and marlin, could store as much, if not more, carbon than some of the largest trees, Pathways had been designated for their protection. "One whale is worth thousands of trees," she remembered reading. *Koholā* and manō *were* the guardians of the climate. And once the manō had learned of these "safe" places, and learned the routes, they had come, and certain individuals, like One and Aka, had stayed.

Kūkia leaned back from the boat deck uneasily. Māihi was being uncharacteristically serious, and he wondered what was wrong. She kept reaching for her hair and drawing up short, and so he didn't tease her as he might have when they were kids. Māihi had cut all her hair off when she lost her husband last year—had kept it short ever since. Still, she clung to the sadness as something integral to her, the way she did her makeup the same way every morning: thick black lines and a rusty-red shadow that made him think of the rust-red dust of Mānā on Kaua'i. She wore her grief with pride.

"We better get going or we'll be late for the ceremony," Kūkia said and took a deep breath of the rain-heavy, salty ocean air. He clapped his hands together in an effort to warm his muscles in face of the *Makani Ōlauniu*—coconut leaf-piercing–wind—and rose from the swim deck.

"Yeah, okay, I—" she started to respond, but her words were cut off by the echo of a motor cutting across the slow-rolling sea's expanse.

"Do they think we're just out here for shits and giggles?" she asked, shaking her head as the boat neared them. There were no boundary lines that you could see, offshore, but everyone knew this was one of the protected Pathways.

The difficulty about guarding something so large that had now grown to trust them, trust this area, was that they were easily found. And that trust, their relationship, meant that many of the manō—One was one of them—greeted the boats, would swim right up to the side of the deck as they did for Kūkia and his ancestors so many generations ago.

"Damn," Māihi swore, and reached for their own steering panel. "I knew it."

"Hold on, Mā," Kūkia said. "What are you going to do when you catch them?"

"You're just going to let them get away with it?" Her voice was deep with the constant sea of outrage she swam in.

"No," Kūkia finally said, glumly. "But if I get shot, I'm blaming you."

As she leapt onto the deck she felt her stomach drop, as though out of her body, to the sound of a gun clicking. There was just one man, and she instantly knew that he was not a fisherman—he looked like someone better suited to be sitting behind a computer screen. She looked the man in the eye without hesitation and, despite her pounding heart and the sweat pooling above her lips, she felt no fear.

"Kū, stay back," Māihi called calmly as she stepped forward, hoping he would listen.

She had known from the very beginning that to bring back the manō, to reclaim these ancestral sea corridors, to put them in 'Ōiwi hands, would inevitably invite violence. It was the cholera epidemic of 1895, the shark culling of the 1960s and 1970s. It was the *make 'īnea*, the anguish-filled deaths of her Hawaiian peoples, their names on waitlists for Hawaiian Homelands, never to be received.

"I'm not here to hurt you. Or to catch you."

She moved toward the man slowly, his hand trembling, finger on the trigger. She could feel, without looking, Kūkia and *The Lanikai* rocking softly behind her.

"You came out here alone?" she asked, continuing to move closer.

"My kids are hungry. My wife is sick. I don't know what else to do," the man finally said, his voice loud and tremulous.

Māihi knew he was telling the truth. "It's okay." She stepped so the rifle was placed firmly against her chest as well as locked into his shoulder where he held it. The rifle's tip was still warm from when he had fired in warning, yet still she felt no fear. "It's okay," she said softly, and she looked clearly into his brown eyes.

After several long moments the man lowered his rifle slowly, as though defeated, ashamed.

"Bring your family to our ceremony today. Bring your wife to our *kahu*. There's plenty of food for your children. My freezer is still full from the October harvest, I have enough to share."

"I'm not 'Ōiwi."

"It doesn't matter."

*

"*Hana hou!*" Kūkia heard over the large speakers as the emcee called for the last performance to be repeated. His eyes were not on dancers but locked on Māihi where she sat, just a pop-up tent away, with her son, August Jr. She was reading something to him, but Kūkia couldn't make out the words over the speaker. She had done her hair and put on a dress since that morning's outing.

"Damn it," he whispered to himself for his curiosity, but he moved to one of the free lawn chairs under her pop-up.

She looked up briefly and gave him a nod but continued to read with her strong, clear voice. "Aloha *kakahiaka*."

Kūkia realized she must be starting from the beginning, as this was the way, in 'Ōlelo Hawai'i, to say good morning.

She continued on in English. Kūkia knew she was still learning how to speak their language. "I am here today to speak on behalf of the manō, our brothers, our cousins, and the *po'e i'a*, the sea people, on which we all depend."

Four-year-old Junior looked up at his mom as though she were Hina and he a pale, lavender *koali'awa* morning glory, drinking in the moon's glow. Everyone called him Junior, as the loss of August still lingered among their people.

Kūkia listened, too, though as *puhi*, eel, emerging from its shade-shrouded coral cave to the bright, dazzling world of the sun-filled open reef. Dazed. Māihi had been asked to give this year's speech at their annual spring equinox ceremony to offer their prayers to restore the climate. The sound of the *pahu* drum moved over the surrounding vendors and family tents, linking their heartbeats in unison.

"We open this ceremony in a place of prayer. We know, as we live the blessings so prayed for by our ancestors, that our place within ceremony, with prayer, moves with and changes our mana: energy, our spirit." Māihi looked up and made eye contact with the two, one pair of eyes young and hungry, the other soft and thoughtful.

"When we ask one another 'How are you doing?' we say '*Pehea 'oe?*' But when we break that phrase apart, and we look at *hea* alone, we know we are calling on, giving name to, to recite, as in genealogy. We recount how we are connected to our ancestors, to our homelands, our homeseas. We are asking of one another's connections to all else. On this tenth anniversary of the Ancestral Seas Pathways program, which makes possible the connected homelands of our manō across Oceania, of our ancestral ways of knowing and caring for the sea, I ask each of you to reflect. What are you connected to? What is your connector to the sacred? And how do you honor it with your life?"

"Mama, can I go get a laulau?" Junior interrupted as she took a breath.

Māihi quickly fished her voucher out of her purse.

Junior ran off with a small skip in his step.

"You know you don't have to be nervous. You're gonna do great," Kūkia told her.

"Can I tell you something?"

"Mmm?"

"I feel like, whenever I'm out in public, everyone is really nice, almost *too* nice, you know? Since August . . ." She didn't like to say it out loud. "And I'm going to be up there, and all anyone's going to see is the sad, lonely widow."

There it was. *August.* Kūkia hadn't known him well; August hadn't grown up with them in Pahoa. Kūkia had only really known him as an amazing sea-person. He had been out picking *ʻōpihi*, highly prized limpets, when he had disappeared. Taken by the Sea.

"You know we've been friends for a long time . . ." Kūkia started. He wished he could hug her, could almost feel her *ʻehu* hair on his fingers as he imagined pulling her tight. "And I promise you, not one of us thinks that.

"You should keep going, I want to hear the rest," he continued.

"Really? You're not just being nice to me?"

"Really."

"Hmm," she said, but she took up the paper again. "*Ke Akua mana loa.* We greet Hina, Kanaloa, and Kāne, the sacred beings we call on to hear our wishes. I pray for the people, for our lives to be good. For the young people, the sick people. We pray for the seasons to be restored, for the wellness of our lives, for fulfillment, for all beings to evade danger, sickness. That we live to become old."

"I need to ask you something," Kūkia interrupted.

"Okay."

"Don't get mad at me?"

"We'll see."

Kūkia knew he was going to regret it before he opened his mouth, but he said it anyway. "You ask in your prayer to evade danger . . . to live to become old."

"Yeah?"

"So, what was that this morning?"

"I don't know what you mean."

"You're willing to . . . die . . . for the manō." It wasn't a question.

Māihi looked out over the vast blue horizon and the foreboding dark gray sea clouds. She chewed her words before she said them. "I think you hit a point where you realize that Death isn't the thing to be afraid of."

"But what would happen to Junior?"

"Gosh, Kū, it's not a big deal," she said with a shallow laugh, as though to brush it off.

"I want you to be serious . . . for one moment. Before you get up in front of everyone and pray for old age." He knew she was going to be so, so mad at him for saying this, and he already wished he could take it back, swallow it somehow. They had known each other forever. And he had loved her forever. And she had chosen August. The constant war raged on in his head. He thought of what her name meant. To peel, or strip, like bark or skin, and depending on its use, to escape . . . by the skin of one's teeth. It was this quality, even from small-kid days, the evasive tenacity, that had drawn him in, had kept them apart.

"He has all of you. All of this," she whispered, her eyes still lost on the Faraway. "That's all I could ever hope for him."

Kūkia had known she was in deep grief, but he had not realized until that morning that she was also standing on *leina's* edge. "He's half August," he said and rose, moving away, toward the elders' tent.

⚶

"Mama!" a little voice called.

Even through the voices and drums, the voice carried, and Māihi knew it was Junior.

Māihi shuffled through the crowds around the hula stage. Everyone was facing the other way, all except for her son, it seemed. She could see his small, sturdy body facing toward the ocean, standing on the high tide line of leaf debris. This was the island point of the Pathway, where land met sea.

"August!" she called sharply, hastening to him. Junior was independent, would only cry out for a real reason.

She was about a hundred feet away when she saw her. Ina's fin was immediately recognizable for the half shred that cut through the stiff half-moon. Ina had been a part of a tagging study many years ago, but the tag had snagged on something and ripped. This was not one of the gentle giants, the whale sharks they had seen this morning. Rather than the distinctive checkerboard pattern of those whale sharks, Ina bore tiger stripes. For some reason, Ina's fin was not moving, but remained lodged in one spot above the waterline. Māihi knew that Ina needed constant movement to get enough oxygen through her gills.

The fear that had been absent that morning pulsed through her now. "Junior," she called. "I want you come to me."

"It's okay, Mama."

He echoed the words she had used that very morning and darted forward into the water, rather than retreat.

She ran after him, for while she loved manō, she also respected them. She dashed the last twenty feet to Junior and entered the water until she was thigh deep, standing between August and the Sea. The waves gently splashed her, trying to knock her off her feet, and she wiped the salt water from her lips.

"What are you doing?" Māihi said softly, trying to keep the fear from her voice. Her hands held tightly onto his shirt behind her.

"Something's wrong with Ina."

Junior had grown up learning about *Kai*, the Sea, from her, but most of all from August. And despite his father's disappearance, Junior had no fear.

"Okay, I want you to go back and get Uncle Kū," Māihi said. He was the kahu manō, the one who would know what to do.

"Mom, there's no time."

"Junior, don't argue with me."

"Mom."

"Fine. You stay right where you are."

"You have to help her."

Māihi looked up at the tormented now-afternoon spring sky, at the incoming surf breaking over the reef beyond. She pushed backward on Junior's chest, forcing him to take a few steps back.

Māihi knew that she could not show fear, but she knew that Ina could feel her heartbeat. She took a deep breath to steady herself.

"*E Kanaloanuiākea,*" she began to sing, remembering the words from Kūkia's tune earlier that morning. *Kanaloa of the vast expanse.*

She waded forward, singing as she went. ". . . *Kanaloa noho i ka moana nui*," she sang, increasing her volume as she moved forward. *Kanaloa residing in the great sea.*

As she moved closer to Ina, now just two feet away, the great body began to move, to thrash with agitation. Māihi was now chest deep, and she could see and feel the presence before her, of a manō that was at least twice her size.

She sang several more lines before she submerged. "*Moana o'o i ka i'a nui, i ka i'a iku, i ka manō i ka niuhi.*" *Mottled sea, in the big fish, in the small fish, in the shark, in the tiger shark . . .* The song directly called on Ina, and as Māihi released that line, she submerged to see what had caught Ina in place.

The thrill of the cool-water shock washed over Māihi, and she blinked as her eyes adjusted to the stabbing salt water. Despite the eddies of fresh water that rippled through and blurred the kai water, Māihi could see that Ina had been caught in a tangled fishing line, stuck in the reef.

Ina's back fin swayed menacingly, but she held a single, smart black eye on Māihi where she appraised her steadily. The intelligence, the pride, was evident.

Okay, Māihi said to herself. *Okay.*

She remained submerged, making sure she knew exactly what they would need, when something tugged on her ankle. With a burst of bubbles, she rose to stand and whirled around to see the source.

"Damnit," she yelped as she locked eyes with Kūkia. She looked beyond him for Junior, relieved to see him on the beach where a small crowd had gathered. More time had passed than she had thought. That was another one of the manō's magics. "You can't do that to me!"

"You kicked me," he said teasingly.

"How are you so calm?"

"You have to be, to be here."

"Well, I'm not."

"Here you are again, twice in one day."

"Hush," Māihi looked at him, already feeling more at ease. She couldn't say it but she felt the calmness that his presence usually brought her. "Did you bring a knife?"

"I brought two," he said, handing her what looked like a kitchen knife from one of the food vendors.

"She's pretty agitated," she said as he wade-swam to be level with her. Māihi wanted to reach out to him, to grab his hand for reassurance, but she held back, her hand curled into a fist instead.

"I'll go around by her head and keep her calm, and you can cut?"

"Kū," she said as he gently lowered himself in the water so as not to disturb the surface. Māihi recognized that, unlike this morning, her body was full of fear. First for Junior, and now for Kūkia. But also, strangely, for herself.

"What is it?" he asked, still calm, steady.

"I'm afraid," she whispered.

"I can do it alone. It's okay."

"That's not what I'm saying!" She twisted her hands tightly. "I know I haven't . . . I know I've been . . ."

"We can do this after," he said, for he could feel his heart pounding now, and he needed to be still within himself.

"Since August . . ."

There it was.

"Sometimes I feel like I've already died."

He gazed at her silently. He knew they needed to get Ina freed, and quickly. But he also knew that this needed to be said in the *before*.

"I'm in love with you," he said simply, flatly, looking away from her toward the horizon instead. He had said it to her in his head a million times before, on a cassette tape that he constantly had to rewind. He had never said it out loud, and he knew he wouldn't have if it were not for the graceful, mana-coiled presence before them, for the death pressed to her chest that very morning.

As the "you" was uttered Kanaloa shifted. Instant, obvious, the small waves that had been pushing against them where they stood, waist high, stopped. The beach had become as a lake—everything was still.

Māihi felt the chicken skin crawl up her arms and breasts. *Holy shit.* She had never seen anything like it. She knew that the Rains, Winds, and Waves listened, knew that very occasionally, they responded. But she had never experienced it for herself. She knew in her whole being that this was not a coincidence.

Māihi reached out for his hand, and he couldn't help but smile. They both submerged together.

Glossary and References

Aloha kakahiaka—morning greeting

akua—deity

E Kanaloanuiākea . . .—composition used to honor Kanaloa

'ehu—reddish tinge in hair, also texture, as salt spray

Hina—deity associated with femininity, moon, tides, the setting sun, healing

"I pray for the people. . . ."—'Ōiwi adaption of *Aatsimoiskaan* (Prayer) documented by Angela Grier, *"Aistimatoom*: The Embodiment of Blackfoot Prayer as Wellness"

Ina—name of specific tiger shark

kai—sea, salt water

kahu—guardian, caretaker (often of the spiritual)

Kanaloa—deity associated with the deep sea

Kāne—deity associated with sunlight, fresh water, rebirth, healing

Ke Akua mana loa—calling on the Great Spirit of great power

koali'awa—beach morning glory

koholā—humpback whale(s)

laulau—Hawaiian dish made of meat, taro, and ti leaves

leina—place where spirits leap into the nether world

Makani Ōlauniu—named wind of the Kona Coast, Hawai'i Island, as documented by our beloved Kumu Roy Alameida

make 'īnea—anguished death

mana—energy, spirit

Mānā, Kaua'i—coastal plain near Waimea on Kaua'i Island

manō—shark

na'au—gut, the place of feeling and intuition

'Ōiwi—Native, native son (Hawaiian)

'Ōlelo Hawai'i—Hawaiian language
One and Aka—names of two of the whale sharks
'ōpihi—Hawaiian limpet that thrives in the intertidal wave zone
pahu—drum
Pehea 'oe?—How are you?
po'e i'a—sea people (inclusive of all marine life)
puhi—eel
The Lanikai—name of their boat
'uwehe—four-count hula dance move

The Blossoming

Commando Jugendstil

A young man, about eighteen years old, give or take, his curly brown hair in disarray and weathered brown skin streaked with dirt, chlorophyll, and scratches, barrels down a steep slope on an electric mountain bike.

Cork oak branches beat him mercilessly as he careens through the trees, bobbing over roots and rocks like a rubber duck in a bathtub.

The young man's eyes are wide and he turns every now and again, cursing under his breath and pedaling even harder, as if all hell has broken loose and all devils are on his trail.

Well, maybe not all devils, but Satanas for sure.

Satanas, the aptly named, bad-tempered stud bull of Seu Nestor, the steward of the neighboring communal *montado*, had been steadily gaining ground with a young cow named Matilda when the human and his vehicle crashed through their secluded grove.

The scare had put Matilda off her mood, and she had left the grove with a haughty swish of her tail, leaving Satanas to nurse his wounded pride.

Not one to spend much time on self-reflection, nor to forgive and much less to forget, the bull had swiftly decided that the best course of action would be to run after the wheeled human and give them a lesson they would not easily forget.

"Go away, you overgrown cow! Go away!" Nuno yells at the top of his voice.

He puts in another burst of speed and dodges between two trees to try and shake off his bovine pursuer.

Centuries of selection for athleticism, fearlessness, and not taking crap from any living being have gifted Satanas with strength, speed, and stamina, but fortunately not with wisdom or the capability to make complex decisions under pressure.

Heedless of anything that is not gaining on his quarry, Satanas charges forward, muscles bunching under his glossy black coat.

He looks like the cover model of a bovine equivalent of *Men's Health*: vigorous, athletic, a bull who doesn't have to ask . . .

And then he ends up stuck between two trees, like an idiot.

Satanas moos and bucks, but he's not great at reversing, among other things. All he can do is watch Nuno slip away between the oaks and the olive trees and simmer in frustration.

The young man lets out a sigh of relief, but it is short-lived.

In his haste to get away from Satanas, Nuno had not noticed exactly where he was going.

A convenient and suspicious pile of wood acts as an almost perfect ramp, and before he knows it, Nuno is flying, arcing high over the fence of a montado and then down a slope covered in loose scree.

The young man screams at the top of his lungs.

By some kind of miracle he manages to keep control of the bike and keep himself on it, bumping and rolling downhill until he finally hits the bottom of the slope and a patch of grass between the trees of another montado, lower down the hill.

He pulls hard on the brakes and puts a foot down for good measure, dragging the bike in a wide arc around that pivot point and opening wide furrows in the grass with the wheels.

Dripping in sweat, he takes a deep breath and pushes his curls away from his eyes with the back of a hand, then lightly pats his jacket.

The flower that can save Neusa's project is still there, in his inner pocket, none worse for the wear.

Satisfied, he takes a deep breath and a moment to examine his surroundings.

The first thing he notices is the sheep.

A lot of sheep, fluffy white or brown, who eye him with interest but without fear, munching their clumps of grass and going "Baa!" between themselves as if holding a conversation he is not privy to.

Nuno feels self-conscious for a moment, worried that perhaps the sheep are making uncharitable comments about the state of his clothes and his hair, or about his cycling moves, as if they have seen better, and then he notices something else.

The shepherdess, mainly.

Hard not to notice her, really.

She looks as tall as a tree and just as wide, the kind of person who could wrestle Satanas into a pretzel or fight a bear for fun.

"You?! Again?!" she roars.

Nuno points at his chest in confusion.

He is sure he's never met this shepherdess before. He would definitely have remembered her if he had, but she doesn't seem to care.

"This is the last time you lot pull this kind of stunt! I will take that fucking ramp and those shitty bikes and make you eat them!" she yells and takes a threatening step forward.

The ground shakes faintly under her feet.

Nuno makes another swift decision and starts pedaling again at full speed.

A quiet, inquisitive "Baa?" resonates throughout the clearing.

A few more "Baas!" answer the first call, and then, in a clanging of bells, the whole herd of sheep starts moving like an organism that trots and clangs and goes "Baa!", united in single-minded pursuit of Nuno's retreating form.

"My sheep! You bastard!" the shepherdess yells in the distance.

"I haven't done anything! Stop following meeeee!" he yells back without daring to turn.

The lead sheep produce a slightly louder chorus of "BAA!" but do not alter their course, pouring down the trail after him like the foam of a carelessly tipped cup of cappuccino.

And how did we get to this, dear readers?

Well, if you have the patience to follow me into this flashback, we will swiftly find out.

Generally speaking, everything started about 13.78 billion years ago, give or take some 20 million years, with a sudden explosion, but, while correct, this fact doesn't add much information to our narrative.

In a narrower sense, everything starts on a Tuesday, March 13 to be precise, at exactly 7:01 a.m. Lisbon time.

The Dawnriders are in the water, just off the beach of Carcavelos.

Even though the rising sea levels of the Late Stage have "drowned" many surfing spots, Carcavelos has been partially spared, so Nuno and his friends are sitting astride their boards, waiting for the next set of waves that is soon to arrive.

In the meantime, they chat, joke, and laugh. Or, rather, they would do so normally.

Today the conversation is a bit more subdued, a bit more serious.

Ana, the oldest in their friend group at almost nineteen, has completed all the learning milestones required for a basic education curriculum and is leaving the Instituto Popular de Saúde Ambiental e Biorremediação, or IPSAB, training programs, where they had all grown up and learned since they were toddlers, to join the Hospital Egas Moniz down in Belém to start her training as a medical professional.

They've all been to the hospital's community learning center for learning activities about the human body and the mandatory first aid courses, but she is going there to stay.

She will even live around there, in a multigenerational housing collective next to the hospital, so she can be fully absorbed in the doctor lifestyle.

This is her last session of weekday surfing for a while, perhaps a long while, but she doesn't seem so sad about it.

She will miss this, and them, sure, but everyone can tell that her sadness is offset by the fact that she can finally, finally reach the shining horizon that she has been chasing her whole life and pursue her vocation full time.

She is almost vibrating with excitement at the idea, and her enthusiasm is infectious.

She is the one with the most solid idea of her future, but most of the others have plans.

João wants to join the Guild of Engineers and learn how to fix people's houses and appliances.

Janice instead is dead set on being a data modeler at the IPSAB and turning piles of environmental data into condensed dashboards that communes, *concelhos*, and *ayuntamientos* across the Iberian Bioregional Federation can use to make informed decisions on the management of the commons.

Fernão and Luciana want to be cooks, or perhaps bakers, and help their grandmother at the local Food Sovereignty and Abundance Guild, and Messias knows he has a berth on his mother's schooner ready for him and has already sailed the trade route to the Caribbean several times as part of his training at the Guild of Navigators of the Grande Lisboa commune.

And finally, Neusa wants to stay at the IPSAB and study the relationship between rare orchids and trees in the montado.

Nuno is the only one who doesn't have a vocation, a plan, or even any real ambition.

He likes the life he's living now, likes to learn and help the IPSAB community wherever and however he can, from kelp-forest restoration projects and field measurements to simply cleaning floors and hauling stuff around.

He doesn't mind lurking on the mutual aid boards for the commune and helping out wherever there is need, but the IPSAB is where his heart is.

The variety of tasks makes him feel like every day could bring new surprises and experiences, the present unfolding before him like a gift, and the knowledge that he is helping understand and restore the rest of nature gives him a sort of satisfaction that he cannot even express.

He knows he doesn't have to change if he doesn't want to.

It's not like in the Late Stage when you had to find a workable, valuable niche and stick to it like a clam on a rock to make a living. There is no obligation to specialize and find one's niche to maximize productivity.

The Universal Basics, things like guaranteed housing, health care, education, and food, ensure that everyone has a good, dignified life no matter whether they can work at all.

People work because they like to, as much as they want to, and a lot of people don't have an old-fashioned career.

Nuno likes what he does and has always imagined he would keep on doing it until he was too frail or sick to continue, but faced with the shining certainty of his friends, for the first time he feels that he might be missing out on something.

He is so immersed in these worries that he completely misses the timing on his next wave and gets thrown off the board, arse over teakettle, and churned up like a rag in a washing machine.

Rookie mistake to try and catch a wave while thinking of something else.

The sea is a jealous mistress. She wants her people's thoughts to be of only her, and she quickly withdraws her favor from those who break the covenant.

Nuno spits out what feels like a liter of water and climbs clumsily back onto his board, head still spinning.

"You okay, mate?" João asks.

Nuno coughs up more water and nods.

"All good," he lies.

João nods back at him and paddles away, lining up for the next wave.

Nuno follows, a bit slower, waiting for the cold water to soothe the bumps he just acquired.

Perhaps he should try out a purpose, just to see how it feels, he reflects. He could just pick one that could work for him and run with it for a while and see if it does something for him.

Role-play it for a bit.

If he is missing something, he will know and will be able to make changes to his life.

He nods to himself again, feeling his inner turmoil evaporate with this decision.

The sea rewards his newfound inner peace with a perfect overhead wave.

It rises unhurried, with stately grace and power, deep green at the base and nearly transparent at the summit, sending rainbows flying in the air from its spray.

Nuno paddles, a frantic burst of movement to intercept the wave, and he can feel the moment when the movement of his board and that of the wave match exactly, and the wave takes over, alive under the wood.

Another burst of motion and he's on his feet, hips twisting, feet shifting, his whole body moving in concert to turn all that energy into motion, a dance back and forth on the edge of the wave, until it breaks on the shore.

The Dawnriders are still complimenting him for his radical ride when they haul their boards back on the *comboio suburbano* toward Cruz Quebrada, hair wet and salty from the sea and sand on their shoes.

✻

Nuno drops his board in the board rack just outside the Department of Agroecology like every morning and climbs up the stairs to the office he shares with the remaining Dawnriders and a bunch of other learners of various ages, grouped by educational milestones.

He checks his messages on the ConvivialNet terminal on his desk. Thankfully, there isn't anything either urgent or important in the inbox, and his next group-learning session on bioremediation isn't until the afternoon.

His groupmate Sunita is holding the weekly presentation on the importance of pill bugs for heavy metal capture.

He was kind of looking forward to that, but now his mind is completely absorbed by his new quest.

He loads up the federated search engine and pulls up a selection of articles from magazines, newspapers, and personal blogs about how it feels to have a calling, a vocation.

He reads fast and takes notes, illegible scrawl spreading all over several virtual sheets of his e-ink pad.

He reads and reads, but none of the feelings these people have for any particular discipline resonate with him.

Undaunted, he pulls up new information, researching the professions most likely to become a calling.

He immediately excludes the religious officer path and the medical professional one. He feels no particular spiritual inclination, and while he likes to help people, he doesn't feel like he would have the stomach for poking in people's innards to do so.

Firefighter is similarly discarded, as Nuno is terrified of both fire and heights.

One by one, Nuno examines and sets aside most of the vocations discussed in his first set of research materials, and by the time Sunita's presentation is due to start, all he's left with are baker and teacher, and the timetables of the baker's calling would require him to drop his dawn surfing sessions.

Teaching it is, then!

Buoyed by the finding, Nuno almost floats into the auditorium and understands maybe half of what his friend is saying, mind abuzz with excitement.

He is going to be a teacher!

Well, at least he is going to try out.

But that's already a start, a direction, and it is more than he had in the morning.

After the peer-learning session, Nuno skips toward the academic advisory and mentorship office.

If the people in there, all permanent or community researchers at the IPSAB, find anything strange in his request to be put in one of the accelerated teacher training programs, they don't say anything, and within a week, Nuno finds himself invited to advanced pedagogy classes at the IPSAB and in other venues across the Greater Lisboa.

He zips to and fro on public transport, his surfskate, and his e-bike, taking part in peer-learning activities about nonhierarchical pedagogy, unschooling, and the facilitation of peer- and group-learning activities for people of different age groups.

There is even a course about how to provide effective mentorship in research and one on how to set up memorable nature-based learning "camps," for example, about permaculture or agropastoralism.

Nuno absorbs everything like a sponge.

He finds everything interesting and enjoyable, but so far there is no spark, no light on the road to anywhere, no epiphany.

Days and then weeks and months pass.

The Dawnriders surf at dawn, but sometimes he has to miss it because the lessons are across town. Likewise, he misses the olive harvest drive because he is busy putting together an educational exhibition on the structure of a food forest along with a group of peers to have it judged by children in the eight- to ten-year-old cohort for clarity, quality, and interactivity.

It's frustrating, but he tells himself that it will be worth it in the end.

Eventually, almost a year into the course, the mentors decree that he is ready enough to tackle some actual educational activities, shadowing more experienced educators.

He arranges things so his placement is in field education and meets his teammates, Luiza and Marina, a pair of sun-browned twin ladies in their forties who will take children on educational foraging trips up the hills over the general holiday between April 25 and May 1.

Buoyant with excitement, he shows up at the now weekly meeting with the Dawnriders at Carcavelos Beach, ready to share the good news with his friends, but as soon as he arrives, he understands that the mood is not quite the right one for a celebration.

Neusa has been crying. She is not crying now, but she must have been until not long before. Her eyes are red and puffy, her cheeks are blotched with red, and she is still making little sniffling noises every now and again and blotting her nose with her flower-printed handkerchief when she thinks nobody is looking.

She tries to pretend that everything is all right and nothing has happened at all, ever, but her attitude doesn't last long when faced with the determined concern of her friends.

"They have destroyed my work," she confesses eventually, sobbing her heart out.

The whole gang has abandoned the idea of a surfing session and sits in a circle around her on the still-cold sand while the tide goes inexorably out, as it is wont to.

The research proposal on orchid symbiosis that she has been working on for the last few years with the help of her mentoring group has just been submitted to the wider scientific community via the federated reviewing portal that links all the Institutos Populares across the world.

"Some folks from the Chiapas and the Cascadia institutes said the project is weak because I didn't have any specimens anymore, and I couldn't be sure I would find others," Neusa half explains, half wails.

Oh, that explains it, Nuno thinks.

When Neusa had started working on that particular kind of orchid-tree relationship, she had a perfect patch of little pink flowers growing around the base of a very old cork oak tree, seemingly forgotten in the middle of a montado up the hills behind Cruz Quebrada.

The little pink orchids sprouting all around her for exactly a fortnight in mid-April were completely unassuming, except for the fact that, somehow, they were one of the very few species of local flowers that formed a mycorrhizal connection with fungi and trees, through the wood wide web, throughout adulthood.

Neusa had been studying that particular tree and its mycorrhizal community for close to three years, and she thought she was close to figuring out why the fungi let the orchid stay connected, and then Grandma Oak was fried by lightning in a winter storm, and the orchids followed her into the great big primary forest in the sky.

And now all Neusa has are half-finished results and no other leads. She is sure that she can find another ancient oak with her little troop of orchids somewhere, given time, but until she does, her rite of passage from student to scholar is in limbo.

By the time Neusa has finished unburdening herself, the sun is already quite high in the sky, and the tide is well out.

The Dawnriders pick up their boards, fold their wet suits back in their backpacks, and disband, but not before promising that they will keep an eye out for ancient trees and for her orchids during any trip to the countryside.

Nuno takes that promise particularly to heart. He'll be traipsing through the montado for a week; he'll have the best chance of finding something, if there is anything to be found at all.

If he didn't have a few days of lessons left before the end of the course, he would just grab his bike and scour the hills top to bottom for them, but he bides his time.

No matter how viscerally he wants to help Neusa, he also needs to focus on his plan. He cannot waste a year and change of trying to figure out whether teaching could be his purpose.

The holiday couldn't come soon enough, though, and finally Nuno finds himself at the bus stop in a little farming village above Queluz, waiting alongside his two mentors for his first batch of students.

He's read the risk assessment, reviewed the plan for their teaching activities, and had a final read-through of his nonhierarchical pedagogy cheat sheet.

He's as prepared as he can be, and yet he cannot help the feeling, not quite fear but also not quite excitement, that tingles down his spine.

It takes a good quarter of an hour of last-minute kit checks and uneasy shifting in place before the school bus arrives, and with it the students.

The kids are about eight to ten years old, very energetic, and mostly interested in what he and the other two educators have to show them.

They ask a lot of questions, examine everything, and make the appropriate oohs and aahs at the right time when shown something cute or cool.

They are all right little humans, and he feels proud of having contributed to kindling or fostering their love of nature.

He doesn't hate the experience. It is quite fun, in fact, and he can see himself doing more of it, every now and again, but once again there is no revelation.

The world doesn't shift on its axis, and he doesn't feel like any extra bit has slotted itself into him, making him see things in a new light, like the materials he had used for research suggested he would.

The montado is a nice place, and the kids and his mentors are cool people, but that's it.

The weight of this lack of realization is so heavy on him that at the end of the workshop, he finds himself sitting on the grass amid the cork oaks, head in his hands.

He is so immersed in his miserable reflections that he doesn't notice that Luiza and Marina have taken a seat on the grass next to him until one of the two (he can't quite keep them straight yet) puts an arm around his shoulders.

"Are you all right, kid?" she asks.

Nuno is determined to bluff his way out and pretend everything is all right, but somehow the words get stuck in the huge lump that has formed in his throat, and, before he knows it, he's started bawling his eyes out like a baby.

Luiza (or Marina, who knows) puts her arms around him and lets him bury his face against her shoulder, while the other twin pats his back reassuringly, murmuring platitudes.

It takes a good fifteen awkward minutes before he calms down enough to stop sobbing, and when he does, all the things he's held inside for more than a year, all the things he's never said to his family, his friends, or his mentors at the IPSAB, come tumbling out of his lips, all at once—a litany of worries, frustration, and feelings of inadequacy.

He hardly knows these two women, and they hardly know him, and yet here he is, letting his heart spill out of him like water from a burst dam.

"Is there something wrong with me?" he wails.

"Of course not, *miudo!*" Luiza (or perhaps Marina) reassures him.

"Then why . . . ?"

Why doesn't he feel like he needs to spread his wings and fly away like his friends?

"See, that is the problem! You assume that because your friends are like butterflies, you must be one too, but not everyone needs a metamorphosis in their lives."

The other twin taps a finger against her chin, deep in thought.

"Every person is different, and it's not like people need a calling to be complete. Being alive and experiencing life is purpose enough, don't you think?"

Nuno cannot help but nod. That's what he's always thought.

"It's just that . . . everybody except Janice and Neusa is leaving, and even they have all of these big plans to specialize and become something else, and I . . . I just want to be plain, old, boring Nuno, helping around at the IPSAB and in town. I am happy as I am."

"If you're happy and you feel like you're living according to your values, you are already in a good place."

Marina (or perhaps Luiza) nods.

"Better than where most people were in our parents' generation, for sure," the other twin agrees.

"And at any rate, if later in your life you find something that you enjoy even more, you can always retrain."

"Yes, like we did. We started out as shepherdesses, but it was too boring, and we were always misplacing some sheep because we were too busy looking at bugs."

"So we did entomology for a bit, but eventually we figured out we liked to teach better than to research."

"So now we're back in the montado, but at least this time we don't have to worry about what the sheep get up to."

Mildly disoriented by the back-and-forth between the twins, Nuno listens and nods. Everything they say makes sense. It makes a lot of sense.

This is no big tragedy, just a minor bump in the road toward figuring himself out. And it's not like he's wasted his time. All the extra training will make him extra useful to the IPSAB and the community of Algés.

In that moment of understanding, it seems to him the skies have gotten clearer, the little birds are singing louder, and the flowers are dancing in the sun and the breeze.

He feels like he's about to break into song like a cartoon princess when his eyes slide once again to an unassuming patch of little pink flowers clustered around an absolutely massive, twisted, and gnarly cork oak.

The sugary pop music soundtrack that was playing in his head scratches to a halt, and he bolts to his feet, fumbling his ConvivialPhone out of his pocket with trembling hands.

He ignores the twins' mildly alarmed questions and checks the flowers against the pictures Neusa sent. He checks them once, and then again, more closely.

It can't be.

The odds are, like, ridiculously low, and yet, somehow these are Neusa's orchids around their grandparent tree.

He tries to steady his shaking hands and takes as many pictures as he can from all sorts of different angles, then harvests a flower and places it in the inner pocket of his jacket.

Neusa might want to have its DNA sequenced to make sure it is the same species as her previous samples.

"I gotta go," he tells the twins.

"You . . . why? What happened?" one of them asks, but Nuno has already jumped on his bike and is barreling downhill at full speed.

"You better come back tomorrow! Do you hear me?" the other yells.

And this, dear readers, is the story of how Nuno ends up racing down the path by the Rio Jamor with a whole herd of overenthusiastic sheep galloping after him.

Entire educational cohorts of coaches and physiotherapists pause in their training at the Jamor National Sports Center to watch him pass.

Several cyclists, runners, dog walkers, and their dogs end up jumping in the river to get out of his path.

Buses and trams honk their horns, people scream and cross themselves, and at least one woman gives birth (correlation, not causation) before this bleating, smelly vision of the apocalypse skids to a halt in the front courtyard of the IPSAB.

Covered in sweat and debris, Nuno jumps off his bike and breaks into a staggering run toward the office.

A few of the bravest sheep try to follow him into the building but are eventually defeated by the automatic doors and a few determined researchers and are left outside to bleat their outrage at being excluded from further adventures.

Blessedly unaware of the standoff between his colleagues and his woolly groupies, Nuno zips down the corridors and up the stairs, scaring the hell out of everyone and causing several health and safety near misses.

He slams open the door to the shared office and, carried forward by his own momentum, crashes to a halt against a desk.

"Nuno! What the hell?! I am in a meeting!" Neusa protests, jumping from her chair, headphones clattering against the worktop.

On the screen a few faces look on, mildly perplexed.

Out of breath and out of steam, Nuno extricates himself from the furniture and shuffles forward on weakening legs.

"For you," he manages to rasp.

The orchid doesn't look like much, especially after what it has been through, but Neusa recognizes it immediately.

She lets out an almighty shriek of delight, and somehow, even though she's about half of Nuno's size, she manages to pick him up and spin him around like a doll.

"You're welcome," he croaks as he slides to the floor.

Neusa straightens up and marches to her triumph, orchid held high.

The people on the other side of the screen look cowed and a bit confused.

Victory is almost assured.

And Nuno? Well, Nuno has just passed out on the floor, back against a desk.

He'll regret it later, but now?

Now he regrets nothing.

Acknowledgments

Imagine 2200 judges
Paolo Bacigalupi, Grace Dillon, Nalo Hopkinson, Arkady Martine, Sam J. Miller, Sheree Renée Thomas

Story reviewers
Leah Bobet, Mimi Mondal, Chinelo Onwualu, Elsa Sjunneson, Sarena Ulibarri

Slush reader
Brianna Castagnozzi

GRIST
Climate fiction creative manager
Tory Stephens

Project directors
Lisa Jurras-Buchanan, Jess Stahl

Acknowledgments

Editors
Chuck Squatriglia, Claire Elise Thompson

Managing editor
Jaime Buerger

Art direction
Amelia Bates, Teresa Chin, Mia Torres

Program coordinator
Josh Kimelman

Author bios

Nadine Tomlinson (she/her) is a storyteller from Jamaica who enjoys writing uncanny tales. Her work has been published in *adda*, *Strange Horizons*, *Lightspeed Magazine*, and other places.

Jamie Liu (she/they) is a writer, climate resilience planner, and climate activism volunteer. She was born and raised in the San Gabriel Valley, California, and currently lives in New York City. This is their first published story.

Susan Kaye Quinn (she/her) is an environmental engineer turned science-fiction writer currently residing in Pittsburgh and dreaming of a better future through her hopepunk climate fiction. Her self-published novels have been optioned for virtual reality, translated into German and French, and featured in several anthologies.

T. K. Rex (they/she) is a speculative fiction author from the western states, whose short stories and poems can be found in more than thirty publications, including *Asimov's*, *Escape Pod* and *Strange Horizons*.

They're an alumni of the Clarion Science Fiction and Fantasy Writers' Workshop, a twenty-year inhabitant of San Francisco, and a friendly acquaintance of spiders. You can find links to their stories and subscribe to their newsletter at tkrex.wtf.

Akhim Alexis (he/him) is a writer from Trinidad and Tobago who holds an MA in literatures in English from the University of the West Indies, St. Augustine. He is the winner of the Brooklyn Caribbean Literary Festival's Elizabeth Nunez Award for Writers in the Caribbean and was a finalist for the Barry Hannah Prize in Fiction and the Johnson and Amoy Achong Caribbean Writers Prize. His work has appeared in the *Massachusetts Review, Transition Magazine, Chestnut Review,* and *Moko.*

Rich Larson (he/him) is the author of *Ymir* and *Tomorrow Factory.* He was born in Galmi, Niger, has lived in Spain and the Czech Republic, and is currently based in Montreal. His fiction has been translated into over a dozen languages, among them Polish, French, Romanian, and Japanese, and adapted into an Emmy-winning episode of *Love, Death + Robots.*

Cameron Nell Ishee (she/her) is a writer and research program administrator most recently based in Vermont whose roots include the Mississippi Gulf Coast. This is the first time her work has been published, and she celebrated with chilaquiles (the best breakfast food).

Sanjana Sekhar (she/her) is a South Indian American writer, filmmaker, and climate activist. Her work amplifies "thrutopian" stories that heal our human relationships to ourselves, each other, and our planet, with a specific interest in radical imagination, sensuality, and solarpunk. She's been featured in the Hollywood Climate Summit, Tedx Climate AcrosstheAmericas, and the Webby Honorees, and she's worked with organizations such as the Center for Cultural Power, Visit California, and the *Washington Post*. She is currently based in LA on Tongva Land.

Louis Evans (he/him) has been going to Passover seder at his Papa and Bubbe's house since he was born. He is a writer living and working in Brooklyn, New York. His science fiction has appeared in *Vice*, the *Magazine of Fantasy & Science Fiction*, and *Nature: Futures*. His climate fiction has appeared in *Analog Science Fiction & Fact*, *Little Blue Marble*, *Fusion Fragment*, and more. He's online at evanslouis.com.

Rae Mariz (she/her) is a Portuguese Hawaiian speculative fiction storyteller, artist, translator, and cultural critic with roots in the Big Island, Bay Area, and Pacific Northwest. She's the author of the Utopia Award–nominated climate fantasy *Weird Fishes* and co-founder of Toxoplasma Press. Her short fiction appears in *khōréō* magazine and on the Imagining Indigenous Futurisms Award short list. She lives in Stockholm, Sweden, with her long-term collaborator and their best collaboration yet.

Gina McGuire (she/her) is an ethno-ecological researcher in Hawai'i, where she considers the well-being of rural coasts from the lens of Hawaiian healing praxis. Her work has been published in *Trouble the Waters: Tales From the Deep Blue*, *Yellow Medicine Review*, Chapter House's *but when you come from water* exhibit, and *Parks Stewardship Forum's* "We Are Ocean People: Indigenous

Author bios

Leadership in Marine Conservation" issue, and she is a winner of the Imagining Indigenous Futurisms Award. Her writing and research are grounded in her love for Indigenous lands and persons (human and nonhuman), and in aloha for her ancestors.

Commando Jugendstil is a collective of solarpunk creators from various disciplines, united in the aim to depict, promote and build sustainable futures. Among the initiators of solarpunk in Italy, the collective has published several short stories in international solarpunk anthologies, taken part in sustainability and public art projects around Europe, and realized a variety of illustrations depicting a future of well-being and abundance for all, such as the postcards published monthly by *Solarpunk Italia* and *Solarpunk Magazine*.

milkweed
EDITIONS

Founded as a nonprofit organization in 1980, Milkweed
Editions is an independent publisher. Our mission is to identify,
nurture, and publish transformative literature and build an
engaged community around it.

Milkweed Editions is based in Bdé Óta Othúŋwe (Minneapolis)
within Mní Sota Makhóčhe, the traditional homeland of the
Dakhóta people. Residing here since time immemorial, Dakhóta
people still call Mní Sota Makhóčhe home, with four federally
recognized Dakhóta nations and many more Dakhóta people
residing in what is now the state of Minnesota. Due to continued legacies of colonization, genocide, and forced removal,
generations of Dakhóta people remain disenfranchised from
their traditional homeland. Presently, Mní Sota Makhóčhe has
become a refuge and home for many Indigenous nations and
peoples, including seven federally recognized Ojibwe nations.
We humbly encourage our readers to reflect upon the historical
legacies held in the lands they occupy.

milkweed.org

Milkweed Editions, an independent nonprofit literary publisher, gratefully acknowledges sustaining support from our board of directors, the McKnight Foundation, the National Endowment for the Arts, and many generous contributions from foundations, corporations, and thousands of individuals—our readers.

This activity is made possible by the voters of Minnesota through a Minnesota State Arts Board Operating Support grant, thanks to a legislative appropriation from the arts and cultural heritage fund.

Interior design by Mary Austin Speaker
Typeset in Adobe Caslon Pro

Adobe Caslon Pro was created by Carol Twombly
for Adobe Systems in 1990. Her design was inspired by
the family of typefaces cut by the celebrated engraver
William Caslon I, whose family foundry served
England with clean, elegant type from the early
Enlightenment through the turn of the
twentieth century.